POWERHOUSE FIVE

by

William Heuman

Ron had to learn a *new* game when he took a job with the Atlas Power and Light Company, after he got out of college. A star basketball player with an engineering degree, he was to coach the Atlas Industrial League team and work in the plant mornings. He found that men who worked all day didn't have the time nor the inclination to practice set plays, as college boys did. In addition, since the men were older than he, they played according to their own rules, which were rather rough, with the referees frequently looking the other way. The team resented his approach and there was a player who undermined his attempts to win games, and so he had many discouraging moments. His great fun was organizing a junior team which kept younger boys busy, too. Here is lots of action and exciting sports, and Ron not only maintained his ideals, but his teammates came to accept them, too.

Classification and Dewey Decimal: Fiction (Fic)

About the Author:

WILLIAM HEUMAN's first literary sale was a juvenile story which brought him $3.50. Since that time Mr. Heuman has contributed articles to national magazines, and written novels and books for young people. He has been an avid sports fan all his life. As a hobby he collects guns and antique weapons. Mr. Heuman lives on Long Island with his family.

Powerhouse Five

WILLIAM HEUMAN

Powerhouse Five

1968 FIRST CADMUS EDITION
THIS SPECIAL EDITION IS PUBLISHED BY ARRANGEMENT WITH
THE PUBLISHERS OF THE REGULAR EDITION
DODD, MEAD & COMPANY
BY

E. M. HALE AND COMPANY
EAU CLAIRE, WISCONSIN

To Don Topliffe

Powerhouse Five

1

Ron Starrett had his first view of the big Atlas Power and Light Company as the train swung around a sharp bend and entered the Willmantic Valley in lower Pennsylvania. It was dusk, and magically the lights from the power supplied by Atlas were beginning to twinkle on like a myriad of stars up and down the fifty-mile-long valley which was bisected by the wide Willmantic River.

At the far end of the valley, along the edge of the town of Willmantic City, his destination, Ron could identify Atlas Power from the huge smokestacks jutting up against the darkening sky.

A conductor moved through the nearly empty car, repeating in a monotone,

"Willmantic, next stop. Willmantic, next stop."

Ron leaned closer to the window, peering out. There were huge plants on both sides of the river, he knew—airplane plants, an enormous guided missile plant, an atomic research laboratory, and other large industrial or steel plants. He was unable to identify each, but immediately after signing on as player-coach of the Atlas Power Company industrial league basketball team Ron had gotten together as much literature as possible on the plant and the Willmantic Valley, because he hoped that he would be having a long and extremely productive stay in the area.

Adam Greer, superintendent of Atlas, had written: "We are not offering you simply a position as player-coach of our representative basketball team. Because of your fine academic qualifications we feel that ultimately we can work you into a highly responsible electrical engineering position with the company. Our basketball team represents us to the public. We are very proud of it and we believe that a man with your background can further develop this aspect of the business."

Coming out of comparatively small Donaldson Tech, and having made the "little" All-American basketball team, Ron had been quite surprised to receive the invitation from Mr. Greer. Coaching and playing in an industrial league team had been the farthest thing from his mind after receiving his degree at Donaldson and spending the summer at a boys' camp and the early fall in New York, working at any temporary job that came along while looking for the right one. He had majored in electrical engineering, and a position with a future at the huge Atlas Power plant was not to be considered lightly. In the correspondence with Mr. Greer, therefore, it had been decided that at first he would spend at least half a day in the plant learning the ropes, and the rest of the time he would devote to basketball.

"Willmantic—Willmantic," the conductor said, passing Ron's seat, and Ron got up, reaching for his bag overhead. Adam Greer had suggested in the correspondence that Ron come to Willmantic on or about the eighth of the month, and Ron had arrived several days earlier because he was anxious to get his feet on the ground, have a look at the plant and the town, and find living accommodations before he went to work with the basketball team.

No one was waiting for him, therefore, when he stepped down from the car with his bags. He was a tall young man of twenty-two, a six-footer, well built, with good shoulders and a trim waist. His brown hair was clipped short and his brown eyes were serious as he moved along the train platform.

From the station agent he learned that the Willmantic House, directly across from the station, was as good as any hotel in town. Willmantic City, Ron had learned from his reading, had a population of some thirty-thousand people, making it a good-sized town, the largest residential area in the valley. This was shopping night in town and the streets seemed to be full of people, with the traffic quite heavy at the main intersection.

In his hotel room Ron unpacked and washed, coming down for supper a half-hour later. As he was passing the desk, the clerk, a youngish man with red hair and spectacles, said to him, "Visiting in Willmantic, Mr. Starrett?"

"I've taken a position with Atlas Power," Ron told him.

"I'll be staying around."

"If you're looking for excitement tonight," the clerk said with a grin, "go over to Union Hall. Your Atlas Turbines are playing an exhibition game with Wheeler Sheet Steel before the regular season gets under way. When the Turbines and the Wheelers get together, things usually start to hum."

Ron nodded and smiled. "I'll drop in and see the game," he said.

Picking up the local newspaper at the desk, he went with it toward the hotel dining room. He was being introduced tonight to a new phase of basketball—the industrial league. This was not strictly amateur athletics. Adam Greer had informed him that while the Atlas team consisted entirely of men on the payroll at the plant, many of the other teams in the league hired out-and-out pros to fill their squads. Probably some of the players would have had high-school experience but little more. Ron was quite curious now to see how well they did on the hardwood.

Atlas, he'd been told, never had had a full-time coach, as one of the players, an older man, had acted in that capacity the previous season. When he'd left Atlas, the position had become vacant.

Willmantic was not a college town. This was an industrial area with no colleges in the vicinity, but it was evidently a hot basketball town and the team Willmantic

City backed was the Atlas Power Turbines, it's alma mater!

While waiting for a table, Ron glanced through the sports pages, noticing first that the writers had given quite a bit of space to the Turbines. From the reporters' accounts it was supposed to be a rough encounter this night, as the Turbines and the Wheelers had put on some rip-roaring contests in the past. Several Turbine players were mentioned by name because of their extreme value to the team, particularly Bo McCloud, who obviously was top cat on the team.

One thought had bothered Ron all the way down to Willmantic, and it had indeed bothered him since he'd agreed to work with Atlas. How would the Atlas players, who probably were some years older than himself, accept a young, ex-collegiate star as their coach and captain? The Turbines were not college men and they might easily resent having a younger man step in to give them orders.

After dinner, Ron inquired the way to Union Hall and then stepped on a bus which took him across town. He walked a half-block to the long, shedlike building where the Turbines played their home games.

Union Hall was a far cry from the various collegiate gymnasiums where Ron had starred in the past. It was a concrete building, almost windowless, with a long oval roof.

The crowds were beginning to pour in, though, when

Ron arrived nearly thirty minutes before game time. This was a different type of spectator, also. There were occasional younger men, and some women and girls, but primarily industrial league basketball was a man's sport, and older men, middle-aged men, seemed to predominate. This was the working class, men from all over the Willmantic Valley, Atlas workers, workers from the nearby airplane and atomic energy plants. The Turbines were their team and they'd come tonight to root them home.

Stepping into the hall, therefore, Ron Starrett sensed a surge of excitement. There was nothing blasé about this audience. They wanted the best team to win, and it had better be the Atlas Turbines!

Union Hall seated about four thousand people in Ron's estimation, and he figured that there were at least three thousand present for this exhibition game tonight.

He found a seat as close as he could to the Atlas bench. The two teams were already out on the floor, the Turbines resplendent in red and white sweatsuits, red jackets with white piping, and the word "Atlas" in white letters across the backs. A diminutive figure of the mythical god Atlas, carrying the world on his back, was sewed on beneath the team name.

The opposing Wheelers were down at the other end of the court, a big team, gaudy in their green and gold outfits with amazing *gold* sneakers. It was quite a bizarre outfit, probably some millworker's idea of real class.

As Ron was settling himself down on the hardwood

bench, a short, middle-aged, stocky man in workman's clothes, heavy Mackinaw, high, laced shoes, and with an orange plastic helmet dangling from his hand, sat down beside him. The stubby man carried a tin lunch box in the other hand. As he sat down, Ron saw the word "Atlas" inscribed on the helmet, and figured that he was probably maintenance crew.

To Ron's amusement, the short man calmly opened his tin lunch box, took out a thermos bottle of coffee and a huge sandwich, and started to eat. Here and there in the audience Ron noticed a number of other men doing the same.

Ron said to him smilingly, "You fellows always bring your lunch to these games?"

The little Atlas worker munched away calmly. "Just comin' off the eight o'clock shift, kid," he said. "We take our time to eat at home, we miss the first half an' we ain't doin' that for nobody."

Ron Starrett was convinced that here were rooters of the most dyed-in-the-wool variety. Even during the warm-up session they were shouting encouragement at the Turbines.

Ron watched with great interest now. There were nine men out on the floor representing the Atlas Power and Light Company, and every one of them was at least a half-dozen years older than himself. Some of the players were closer to ten years older! One rather short fellow with powerful legs actually was semibald.

It was not a particularly tall team as basketball squads went these days, and Ron was glad for this. He liked men who could travel on the court, and some of the men in the red sweatsuits seemed really fast.

The Turbines did have one big man, probably the center, a red-haired, freckle-faced chap of about twenty-eight who was at least 6′7″ and had plenty of spring in his legs.

Without asking, Ron tried to pick out Bo McCloud, star of the Turbines. He looked over the nine men carefully and decided upon a black-haired, black-jowled Irishman with a pug nose and a piece of adhesive tape across his right cheekbone. The Turbine player had a tough chin and pale blue eyes. He was about Ron's height, an even six feet, but a little heavier in the shoulders. He had a very nice touch as he lifted the ball up toward the rim on the practice shots.

As the chubby Atlas maintenance man was pouring himself a cup of hot coffee, Ron said to him, "Which one is McCloud?"

"Number 3," the Atlas worker told him, and Ron grinned. Number 3 was the Irishman with the patch. "Big fellow is Stretch Moynihan," the Atlas rooter went on. "Number 2, dark-haired guy, is Rocco Sterovitch, an' nobody better push Rocco around on the court tonight."

Ron had noticed the Number 2 man, a dark-haired, powerfully built Pole with a slag of a jaw. Sterovitch had arms and shoulders like a weight lifter and he, too, was fast.

"Small, baldy feller," Ron's informant said, "is Bennie Andrews. He ain't near as old as he looks, an' he can move with that ball."

Ron watched Andrews going in with a lay-up and he was convinced that he could do exactly what the Atlas man said he could do.

"Number 4 man is Jig Mackey," the Atlas worker said. "Best floorman on the team—ball handler, feeder." He paused and looked at Ron and he said. "You new in town?"

"I'm new," Ron nodded.

"Turbines got a new kid comin' down from college," the Atlas worker said expansively. "Supposed to be a whiz-bang, All American, or somethin' like that. Read about it in the company paper. Hear he's gonna coach this club. I'm tellin' him right now he'd better not try to coach guys like Bo McCloud an' Rocco Sterovitch too hard."

Ron Starret looked out over the court thoughtfully. He was wondering about that, himself, as he sat on the hard-wood bench now. What kind of tigers would he have in his cage!

2

The game got under way a few minutes later and Ron leaned forward in his seat as the Turbines went through their paces. It was a good team, fast, experienced, a much better team than he'd anticipated. As a matter of fact, after watching them for only a few minutes, he was convinced that either one of these teams could have taken his Donaldson Tech and most of the smaller collegiate fives against which he'd played.

He did notice that the Turbines were a trifle sloppy on their pick-offs and screens, and he would have to work on those weaknesses as coach. Also, they weren't using any set plays whatever.

Back at Donaldson, the very astute veteran coach, Jim Milligan, had always believed in a few simple set plays, especially something coming out of out-of-bound balls, and Ron planned on introducing these plays to the team.

As he and the crowd had anticipated, it was a rather rough, bruising game with plenty of body contact, with the referees being quite lenient in their calls. It was not a dirty game, but, under the basket, fighting for possession of the rebounds, there were wild-swinging elbows and knees, and neither team seemed to shy away from them.

As Ron had also anticipated, the two top men on the Turbine squad, McCloud and Sterovitch, were right in the middle of the roughhouse. Before the game was five minutes old, McCloud and a Wheeler player were having words and the heavily partisan Turbine crowd was urging Bo to "take him apart."

The referees, both big fellows, cool, experienced, seemed to know exactly what to do in a situation like this, and they moved in between the two players, breaking it up.

There was no ill feeling, though, between McCloud and the Wheeler man. The redoubtable McCloud seemed to know the other man pretty well and, as they walked away from each other after being warned by the referee, Bo shook a finger scoldingly at the tough redhead with whom he'd nearly tangled.

Industrial league games were played in four periods and, by the second period, the Turbines led by a 24-19 score, with McCloud high man, having dropped in four field goals, one of them a beauty coming on a tap-in.

Bennie Andrews was doing well for himself, also. Despite the balding head, Andrews was all over the court, moving constantly, running at different rates of speed. When he broke for the basket, going after a feed pass, and he let out all the stops, he could really move.

Under the basket big Stretch Moynihan was having a time with the Wheeler center, a giant by the name of Abe

Kindred. It was clean play, but rough, as rough as Ron had ever seen it, with both men maneuvering for position, trying to get the advantage.

There was very little whistle-blowing in this game, the referees and league officials having apparently accepted the fact that it was a rough game with rough men playing it. They maintained order on the court and they never let the game get out of hand, but a good deal of body contact was permitted.

At half-time the Turbines led by a 48-44 score, with McCloud high man with eighteen points. The little Atlas employee beside Ron said,

"Guess old Adam Greer's gonna be happy tonight, fella."

"Is Mr. Greer in the hall?" Ron asked curiously.

"Never misses a game," the Atlas worker said. "Sittin' right down there behind the bench."

Ron had noticed a rather big man with heavy shoulders and graying hair sitting directly behind the Turbine bench up ahead. He'd noticed, also, that Mr. Greer was not alone. A dark-haired girl in a trim, tan suit sat with him. When she turned her head on one occasion he noticed, too, that she was quite nice looking, her nose well shaped, a slight upturn to it.

"The girl Mr. Greer's daughter?" Ron asked.

The Atlas man chuckled. "Can't blame you for noticin' her, son," he said. "That'll be Millicent Brown. Handles public relations now that Joe Hanson is away on sick leave. That kind of puts the basketball team in her department."

Ron thought about that. An industrial league basketball team could be considered to be under the jurisdiction of the public relations department, as the team presented an image to the public. He found himself wondering idly how much contact Miss Millicent Brown *did* have with the Turbines.

The players from both teams had left the floor now and Ron got up from his seat and made his way out to the aisle. He went down the stairs, coming up behind Adam Greer where there were now some empty seats, and he said, "Excuse me, Mr. Greer."

The Atlas superintendent turned, and he had the bluest eyes Ron had ever seen, a very penetrating blue which went well with his steel-gray hair. His jaw was tough and uncompromising. After one close look at him, Ron was convinced that this was a man who would not be pushed around by anyone.

"My name is Starrett," Ron told him. "I just got in this evening."

For one moment the name didn't register, and then suddenly Adam Greer smiled warmly, his whole face changing as he did so. "Of course—of course," he said. "Starrett. You're here a few days early, aren't you?"

"I wanted to look over the town and the plant before I started work," Ron explained.

"Good idea," Adam Greer nodded. Turning to the girl

at his side he said, "Millicent, this is Mr. Starrett, our new basketball coach. You will remember we've been having some correspondence with him. This is Miss Brown."

"Yes," Millicent said with a warm smile. "I'm glad you've decided to come to Willmantic, Mr. Starrett." She held out her hand and Ron shook it cordially. She had brown eyes to go with the brown hair, very nice brown eyes.

"Join us," Adam Greer invited. "Now what do you think of our team? I presume you've been watching the first half?"

"I've been watching," Ron answered, "and they're good, real good. As a matter of fact, they play a much better brand of basketball than I had expected."

Adam Greer smiled as if pleased with the statement. "These fellows have been around a long time," he said, "but I think what they need now is someone to polish off the rough edges. I'm sure you're the man to do it, Ron."

"I hope so," Ron told him. He added. "I realize that most of these men are somewhat older than myself, Mr. Greer, and more experienced in many ways. I hope I don't have any difficulties from the coaching end."

"It's your team," the Atlas superintendent told him quietly. "You handle it the way you wish. I am glad to hear you speak this way, though. I was afraid you might turn out to be one of those brash young men who look down their noses at our industrial league teams."

"If I ever look down my nose at a fellow like Mc-Cloud," Ron said with a grin, "I might *lose* it! He's rough —rough but very good."

Millicent laughed and it was good to hear her.

"McCloud's all right when you get to know him," she said. "He just doesn't like anybody stepping on him on the court."

"I noticed that," Ron chuckled.

"We'll meet the team after the game tonight," Adam Greer was saying. "I believe I wrote to you, Ron, that we open the season officially next Monday night against the Pittsfield Ironmen."

Ron watched with interest as the Turbines came out on the court a short while later. He said to Millicent, who was sitting next to him, "All of these players are actively employed by Atlas, I understand."

"The whole squad," Millicent said. "We prefer it that way. McCloud and Moynihan work with maintenance crews. Sterovitch is in the pump room. Bennie Andrews works in the control room, and Jig Mackey is a turbine operator."

Ron had noticed Mackey on the floor that first half. He was a tall, rangy, good-looking fellow with jet black hair parted in the middle, and odd green eyes. Mackey seemed to be the playmaker of the team. He didn't have McCloud's or Sterovitch's drive but he was the smoother ball handler, setting up many of the plays with his deft passes. Several times Ron had noticed him speaking with some of the players as if giving them instructions or tipping them off about something.

"As far as the team is concerned," Mr. Greer was saying, "we practice occasional evenings in the high-school gym in town when it isn't being used. Since Johnny Bianco left us last year we haven't been working out with any regularity but I'm sure you'll want to start a few workouts as soon as possible."

"I'd like a practice session or two before the Pittsfield game," Ron agreed.

The third period got under way with the Wheelers anxious to catch up. There was more rough play with both teams hitting hard under the baskets. Sterovitch was a bear-cat on the rebounds. Although only a six-footer, he seemed to have steel springs in his legs and he could go as high as the big men, and higher.

The Wheelers came to within two points of the Turbines and then McCloud and Moynihan hit for five successive baskets. Mackey dropped in two set shots from outside, a speciality with him, and the game was in the bag.

McCloud, acting as captain and coach, threw in a few utility men near the end to give the regulars a breather. It was 91-84 for the Turbines at the finish, and the big crowd seemed quite happy as they filed out of Union Hall.

Millicent Brown parted with Ron and Mr. Greer out in the lobby, because the two men intended to visit the locker room.

"See you in the office," she said, smiling, and Ron was quite sure that he would and as often as possible! He didn't remember when he'd been so impressed with a girl. And they were working practically in the same department in the company which made it even nicer.

3

The hard-bitten Turbines had just entered the dressing room when Ron walked in with Adam Greer. They were sweaty and bruised from the rough conflict with the Wheelers. All of them looked at Ron curiously as he came in. Besides the regulars there were four other utility players in the room.

"Boys," Adam Greer said, "I want you to meet the new Turbine coach, Ron Starrett."

Bo McCloud turned and stared at Ron. He was pretty much the same height and build as Ron, but about six years older. They were, however, as different as a rhinoceros and a horse. Ron was the clean-cut college boy, nicely dressed, clean shaven. McCloud was the typical hard-faced millworker.

Turning around he put his back against the locker and he said softly, "How's it?"

There was a kind of grin playing around the corners of his mouth and, noticing it, Ron Starrett's brown eyes hardened slightly.

Rocco Sterovitch had been standing in front of a small mirror on the wall, looking at a cut on his cheek. He turned around now, smiled rather contemptuously, and nodded.

Stretch Moynihan on the rubbing table just scratched his chin.

Bennie Andrews said, "How do you do?"

It was all the greeting Ron received.

"Congratulations on a fine game tonight," he said quietly, and then he went around from man to man, shaking their hands.

Rocco Sterovitch said soberly, "My hand's got dirt on it, kid."

The only man who greeted him with real politeness, besides Andrews, was Jig Mackey, who said, "Good to have you with us, Ron."

Adam Greer was frowning, having noticed the unveiled contempt in the eyes of most of the players. He said, "Do you have anything you'd like to say to the team, Ron?"

Ron nodded. He'd captained the Donaldson Tech team for two years and he'd become accustomed to acting in a leadership capacity. Now he said, "I understand we open the season next Monday against Pittsfield. If I may, I'd like to call a special practice session for Thursday night to get acquainted with the squad."

McCloud said languidly, "You may, Mr. Coach."

Rocco said from the mirror, "You figure on playin' with this club, too, Starrett?"

"I expect to play," Ron nodded.

McCloud said, "You might find our kind of basketball

a little different from what you been playin' back in college, kid."

Adam Greer seemed about to take exception to Bo's attitude toward the new coach but before the Atlas superintendent could say anything, Ron said evenly, "I'm willing to find out, McCloud."

"An' you'll find out." McCloud grinned.

As Adam Greer started to speak, Ron said quickly, "That'll be all, gentlemen. I'll see you on Thursday. Good night."

When they were outside Mr. Greer said tersely, "I wasn't too pleased with their attitude, Ron. I've a good mind to go back inside and put them in their places. These men are working for Atlas and representing us. Every one of them is being paid an extra bonus to play basketball for the company."

"I'd rather you wouldn't speak to them," Ron said. "I think I can handle it myself, once we're working out on the court." He added with a smile, "I was afraid they wouldn't take me too seriously as player-coach, Mr. Greer."

"In other words," Adam Greer nodded, "you want to prove yourself, Ron?"

"That's about it," Ron told him, "and the sooner the better."

He was anxious to be out on the court now and get the feel of the ball. After the summer at the boys' camp he was still in excellent physical condition, having participated in many of the activities of the camp, and this included basketball. However, in the past weeks in New York, after the camp closed, he hadn't touched a ball.

Adam Greer said quietly, "if they give you a hard time, Ron, I want you to tell me."

"If they give me a hard time," Ron observed, "and I can't handle it myself, I don't belong here, Mr. Greer."

He saw the satisfied smile come to Adam Greer's face. "I think you'll do, Ron," the Atlas superintendent said. "Good luck."

The next morning at eight o'clock Ron entered the main office of the Atlas Power and Light Company, and the first person he saw coming along the hall was Millicent Brown. The girl stopped immediately, smiling, and she said, "You're an early riser, Mr. Starrett."

"There'll be a lot to see down here," Ron told her. "I thought I'd get a good start."

"I'll show you to Mr. Greer's office," Millicent volunteered, "and do drop in to mine occasionally. The basketball team is listed under public relations, and we may be able to work something out to publicize it a little more."

"Thanks for the invitation." Ron smiled, feeling that the day was starting out right.

One of the company engineers, a short, pudgy man by the name of Ormsby, took Ron on a tour of the plant. Atlas Power and Light was enormous, the main building spreading over many acres of ground with a half-dozen huge smokestacks reaching toward the sky.

Across from the main plant lay the transformer yard, from which the current was shot up and down the long Willmantic Valley. As Ron was crossing to the yard with Ormsby, an orange maintenance truck with a half-dozen crew men in it rolled by slowly. One of the men in the truck yelled, "Hey, Mr. Coach, how's it?"

Ron looked up and saw Bo McCloud in workmen's clothes and orange helmet standing in the back of the truck, grinning at him. Stretch Moynihan, a pole-climber's belt around his waist, stood next to him, the helmet pushed back on his head. Lifting a big hand, Stretch called softly,

"Good morning, dear coach."

Ron grinned, also, and waved back at him. The other maintenance men in the truck were guffawing loudly.

Ormsby said, "They're a rough bunch, Starrett. Don't let them get under your skin."

"They won't," Ron assured him.

Down in the pump room they ran across Rocco Sterovitch on duty among the maze of pipes, pumps, motors and fans which were required to keep the big turbine-generators in action. Rocco waved but didn't try to talk because of the steady roar and hum of the motors.

In the control room Bennie Andrews sat at one of the huge panels. It was quiet and air conditioned in here, and Bennie, an older man who obviously was not going to get on Ron's back, said cordially, "What do you think of it, Starrett?"

"It's tremendous," Ron told him with enthusiasm, and he saw the appreciative smile come to Bennie's face.

"Glad you like it," Bennie smiled. "We're kind of nuts about it, too."

"Mr. Starrett has an electrical engineering degree," Ormsby said, "and I suppose he's as much interested in the plant as he is in the basketball team. Isn't that right, Ron?"

"I intend to make a career out of engineering," Ron assured him.

Ormsby said. "We burn gas and oil at this plant, generating great quantities of steam in the boilers. The steam is passed through the turbines, revolving the turbine wheels which in turn rotate the shaft of the generator where the electricity is being produced. The current then passes into the conductors under the floor and crosses to the transformer yard where it is given a boost so that it can reach the farthest ends of the valley."

"And Atlas supplies the entire valley," Ron said.

"Every bit of it," the engineer stated. "We are one of the largest plants in the east. There must be three dozen companies in the valley dependent upon Atlas for power and light."

In the turbine room they met Jig Mackey at the control panel. Mackey watched them coming up, nodded, and smiled. The loud hum of the turbines where Jig was located made it impossible to talk, but as they were leaving the room and heading for the elevators which would take them to the boiler room, Ormsby said, "A good man, Mackey, a company man. Everybody likes him."

"Quite a basketball player, too," Ron observed.

Back in the main office about noon, Ron saw Millicent Brown heading down the corridor in his direction. She was wearing a jacket and was obviously going out to lunch.

"How was the tour?" Millicent asked, slowing down as she neared him.

"My head's spinning," Ron smiled. "It'll take some food and drink to get me out of orbit." He added hesitantly, "Do you feel the same way?"

"I was going to lunch," Millicent said with a laugh, "if that's what you're asking."

"I'm new in town," Ron told her. "You might know a good place."

"I might," Millicent agreed.

They had an excellent luncheon in a small restaurant in town, Millicent driving them down in her small compact. As they sat across from each other, Ron said curiously, "You're rather young to be heading a public relations department, Millicent."

"Not really heading it," she explained. "I'm Mr. Hanson's assistant, but he's on sick leave. I've always lived in Willmantic City and I took up public relations at State University." She changed the subject deftly. "I understand you're an All-American basketball player, Ron. I used to watch all the games at the university."

"I was picked on some of the *little* All-American teams," Ron corrected her. "There's quite a difference, you know."

"You mean they're *small* players?" Millicent asked him archly, and then both laughed.

"Making the real All-American squad is quite an accomplishment," Ron told her. "At Donaldson we never played the kind of competition you had at your alma mater."

"Don't be so modest," Millicent reproved him. "You were highly regarded as a basketball player. That's the reason Mr. Greer asked you to come out here."

"I'm kind of glad I came, now," Ron said.

"I'm glad you came, too." Millicent smiled as she spoke, looking right at him.

Ron Starrett was thinking that it was this that he liked about her. She was honest. There were no pretensions. He was positive now that Willmantic City was where he wanted to settle down, and for more reasons than one!

4

The next night in the Willmantic High School gymnasium dressing room, Ron got into his Turbine uniform and went out on the court with a basketball. He was the first man on the floor as the other nine men on the squad were still changing.

Wearing his sweat jacket, he took a few easy shots at the rim, following with lay-ups. He handled the ball nicely; he had a deft touch and he was fast on his feet for a man over six feet tall.

Now the other Turbine players straggled out of the locker room, moving toward the basket where Ron was taking his shots. Bo McCloud carried a ball with him, and now he very awkwardly cocked his head and pushed it toward the backboard the way a rank amateur would. The ball bounced off the board, not even coming near the rim, and McCloud said mischievously, "That the way you do it, Mr. Coach?"

Rocco Sterovitch said, "Are all basketballs *round,* Mr. Coach?"

Ron smiled. He called for the other ball and then holding both balls under his arms he said, "We'll start with a warm-up session. Lay-ups down the left side, then down the right side, and finally down the middle. Five times each way. We just want to loosen up."

Stretch Moynihan said, "Ain't that ducky!"

They lined up, though, and they made a farce out of it, Ron watching them, a very faint smile on his face. They were like a bunch of small unruly boys on a holiday and in a sense it was *funny*.

Bo McCloud made a pass back between his legs to Rocco Sterovitch, and then he yelled, "Ain't you gonna play with us, Mr. Coach?"

"Pretty soon," Ron told him.

He didn't care whether they made the shots or not. This was just a warm-up session to work up a little sweat.

The only man who didn't cut up was Jig Mackey. Mackey seemed to be the outsider on this team. It wasn't that the players didn't like him or held any resentment against him, but Mackey just didn't seem to be part of the group at all.

McCloud kept saying, "When are *you* gonna play with us, Mr. Coach?"

It was becoming obvious to Ron that these fellows wanted to get him into a scrimmage where they could work him over. In their eyes he was still the college boy, fresh out of school, playing a namby-pamby type of basketball.

"We'll have a little scrimmage later," Ron assured McCloud.

"Hear that!" Bo whooped. "We're gonna have a little scrimmage, men. We gonna have tea served after the scrimmage, Mr. Coach?"

There was a roar of laughter from some of the players, but Ron only smiled. He was anxious, himself, to work out with the team, to be actually in competition with them and get the feel of the action. That was the only real way to gauge the worth of a basketball player—to be on the floor with him, take his passes, watch him cut.

After ten minutes of warming up Ron said, "All right, men. We'll make up two teams—the five starters and the utility men. I'll work in with the second squad."

Bo McCloud said immediately, "I wanna play on the coach's side."

"Me, too." Rocco Sterovitch grinned.

"Let's go," Ron told them. He took the ball out of bounds underneath one of the baskets as the five regulars moved back, each preparing to pick up one of the utility men as they came upcourt.

Ron bounced the ball to George Kramer, one of his four utility men, and then he moved upcourt, not too surprised to see Bo McCloud pick him up because he'd anticipated this. McCloud wanted to show him up tonight.

"Now don't go too fast," Bo warned. "We ain't used to runnin' fast around here, Mr. Coach."

Ron didn't say anything. He ran upcourt easily, crossed, and took a pass from Doug Maceo, handing it to Chuck Abrams. Then he continued under the basket, McCloud going with him.

Ron wasn't quite prepared for what happened next. He tried to make a quick cut in toward the center, but McCloud suddenly moved directly in front of him so that the two men collided.

"Oops!" McCloud gasped. "I didn't see you comin', Mr. Coach."

Ron said nothing, but the smile had left his face for a moment.

He'd been moving easily on the court but now he suddenly opened up, cutting left toward the basket. He'd always been tremendously fast on the break and he was really moving, getting good distance between himself and the surprised McCloud.

George Kramer, seeing him in the clear, whipped the ball to him, and Ron, taking it on the dead run with one hand, transferred it to the other as Rocco Sterovitch switched over to pick him up. He went up high with his left hand, going even higher than Sterovitch, pushing the ball above Rocco's fingertips and netting it very cleanly.

"Hey!" Bo McCloud yelled. "You forgot to wait for me, Mr. Coach."

"Next time," Ron smiled.

"That's what you think," McCloud told him.

The regulars came upcourt with the ball now, Ron picking up McCloud, moving back with him. He'd watched Bo against the Wheelers and he had a pretty good idea what the Turbine captain could do.

"Don't play me too close," Bo said as he drifted around underneath the basket. He took a pass from Andrews and flipped it out again to Rocco. Then he crossed the court, Ron staying with him, waiting for the fast break, confident that he could keep up with the man.

Now McCloud cut, taking the pass from Jig Mackey, but again Ron was with him, forcing him toward the outside away from the basket, and McCloud had to fire the ball back to the center.

He cut again with Stretch Moynihan giving him a bounce feed pass, but this time Ron moved in front of the ball, slapping it away from McCloud and picking it up all in one motion. In a fraction of a second he was speeding upcourt, breaking out into the clear with his dribble, whipping the ball to little Doug Maceo, a brown-skinned Italian.

Doug, cutting in from the side easily, made the two-pointer and then let out a whoop of satisfaction. It had been a very nice play and both McCloud and Moynihan looked discomfited.

"So," McCloud said, "you're gonna play it tricky, are you, Mr. Coach?"

"You boys shouldn't let those bounce passes hang," Ron told him. "Keep them short and fast."

Stretch Moynihan frowned at him.

The regulars came upcourt again, this time with McCloud determined to show Ron up. He wasn't smiling any more, knowing that so far in this game he'd been outplayed by the ex-collegian.

The regulars worked it fast, a little too fast, and a pass got away from Bennie Andrews. Larry Sauer of the utility squad picked up the ball and fired it across to Ron.

"Go!" Ron yelled.

The utility men broke toward the basket and he whipped the ball to Doug Maceo. Getting it back he slammed it to George Kramer who was cutting for the board. Kramer missed the two-pointer, the ball rolling off the rim, but Ron, streaking down the middle after the shot, went up high, got his fingertips on the ball and gently nudged it back through the net for his second field goal.

"O.K., wise guy," Bo McCloud growled.

Doug Maceo whooped, "We're killin' 'em! We're killin' the regulars!"

They didn't kill them too long, though, because the first-string men, buckling down to business, started to score. Moynihan hit from the bucket; Bennie Andrews came in with a lay-up. Mackey hit from the corner, but Bo McCloud failed to get loose.

As the minutes went by Ron realized that this fact was becoming more and more annoying to the tough Turbine captain. Ron played him close all the way, forcing Mc-Cloud always to the outside where he couldn't get off his shots.

On one occasion Ron tore down the middle on a driving lay-up, the first one he'd attempted, and McCloud hit him the way a hockey player uses a shoulder block. Ron got the ball off, however, up and over McCloud, and it was another field goal.

McCloud said tersely, "Just watch that rough stuff, kid. I don't like guys chargin' in like that."

"I had a free lane," Ron told him. "You blocked it up. The foul would have been on you, Bo."

"Oh, yeah?" McCloud said grimly. "Says who?"

Ron moved away from him, giving him no answer, and he could see from the contemptuous expression on McCloud's face that the Turbine captain thought he was afraid.

Now with Ron warmed up and taking charge on the court, the utility men played surprisingly good basketball. Ron had always been the playmaker at Donaldson, the man who moved the ball and kept it moving. He was the take-charge guy on the court and the Turbine players with him sensed this fact immediately. He set the tempo, he maneuvered the play, and usually he made the key pass.

McCloud made his first basket when Ron switched to pick up Bennie Andrews, but then Ron came back quickly with another two-pointer, swinging in from the corner and taking Larry Sauer's bounce pass. He'd had a half-step on Bo this time, faking him off-balance with a shift of the shoulder.

McCloud went up with him to the rim on this one, hacking hard at him, but Ron got the ball free. McCloud wasn't laughing any more now, and with each passing minute his game grew rougher. Once he charged Ron from the side as Ron was dribbling downcourt and he literally knocked the coach out of bounds with the ball.

Smiling, Ron said, "Take it easy, Bo."

He made no attempt to retaliate. He still played the Turbine star very closely, moving with him on the break for the basket. In desperation on one occasion Bo piled down the middle, driving straight into Ron on a move which surely would have drawn a charging foul against him.

McCloud lost possession of the ball but instead of going after it he stepped up to Ron and pushed him back hard with both hands.

The play stopped on the court automatically and the eight other men waited, supposing that Ron would make an attempt to get back at McCloud, or at least remonstrate with him. McCloud's act had been a deliberate challenge, an invitation to Ron to defend himself.

Instead of charging back at McCloud with both fists, Ron simply picked up the basketball and bounced it, his face expressionless. He said quietly, "That'll be all this evening, gentlemen. I'd like you to work for a while on your foul-shooting. I noticed you were a bit weak against the Wheelers."

They all stared at him and even the four utility men with whom he'd been playing almost brilliant basketball turned away in contempt. McCloud, himself, just looked at Ron grimly, but made no attempt to follow up his first rash action. He turned away and Ron appreciated this move. McCloud had shown up his man, thought him a coward, but had no intention of further bullying him. It was a good quality to see in the tough Turbine captain.

The remainder of the practice session was dull, indeed. None of the players tried to poke fun or jibe at the new coach. They'd seen him in action and they'd found him wanting, or at least that was the conclusion they'd reached. He could play basketball and he could play it well, but there was something missing in his make-up. He'd been pushed around and he hadn't fought back, and in industrial league play this was an unpardonable sin.

5

After the men had worked on their foul-shooting for about half an hour Ron said, "That'll be all, gentlemen. It was a good session."

Rocco Sterovitch spoke for the whole squad. "Was it, kid?" he asked sourly.

They stalked into the locker room, and Ron, retrieving the basketballs, followed them. He took the balls to a bin in the school gym office and then he crossed to a second bin nearby which he had noticed earlier contained two pairs of eight-ounce boxing gloves.

Hefting them in his hands thoughtfully for a moment, he stepped out of the office, carrying the gloves, walking down between the rows of lockers toward the shower room near where the Turbine players were changing.

Bo McCloud sat on a bench, wiping his face with a towel. Rocco Sterovitch was on the same bench a few feet away, pulling off his sneakers. Big Stretch Moynihan was in the act of opening a locker when Ron appeared with the two pairs of boxing gloves.

McCloud looked up, surprised, when Ron stood in front of him. Ron said, "Like to put these on, McCloud?"

He held out a pair of the wine-colored boxing gloves.

Bo McCloud stared, and Rocco Sterovitch gulped and said, "What's this?"

Ron said, "Thought you might like to try these on, McCloud. I'll be waiting for you out in the gym."

He dropped the boxing gloves into Bo McCloud's lap and he walked off, swinging the pair he carried and humming gently to himself. He heard Stretch Moynihan say behind him, "For cryin' out loud!"

Rocco Sterovitch said, "Bo will kill the kid! It'll be murder!"

Moving out onto the gym floor, Ron heard the quick buzz of voices behind him. He closed the door, crossing the gym to a corner where there was a heavy punching bag and a light bag.

Pulling the gloves on his hands he started to hit the heavy bag a few light blows when the Turbine team trailed out onto the court. McCloud was carrying the gloves. He hadn't put them on as yet.

McCloud was smiling when he came up, a tough smile. "What's the matter, you crazy, kid?" he asked. "You wanna be killed?"

"They're eight-ounce gloves," Ron observed. "I don't think anybody's going to be killed." He held his own gloves out to Stretch Moynihan and he said, "You mind tying the laces, Stretch?"

Moynihan looked at him and then at McCloud, and he shook his head, but he started to lace the gloves.

Rocco Sterovitch shrugged and said, "So he wants it, Bo, give it to him. It ain't somethin' you started."

It *was* something Bo McCloud had started and Bo knew it, and now Ron could see that he was a little ashamed of himself for forcing a fight like this. McCloud, who'd evidently had his share of rough and tumble encounters, actually was afraid of hurting the new coach!

"O.K.," Bo said reluctantly. "You want to fight, kid, I guess I'll have to fight you."

"Box," Ron corrected him. "I never fight, Bo."

Bo glanced at him. "So you're a fancy boxer," he said. "That's all the better, kid. It might not be so bad."

Rocco laced the gloves for the Turbine captain and then Bo moved out onto the court where there was room to maneuver. The Turbine players watched without a word as Ron followed him, punching at one glove with the other, his face expressionless.

Physically, they were quite well matched, but McCloud seemed the more rugged man even though he did not weigh five pounds more than Ron. At Donaldson Ron had weighed in at 185 when he'd worked out with the boxing team. He weighed 187 now, and he had good sloping shoulders with plenty of punching power in them, a trim waist, and fine tapered legs.

He stood in front of McCloud, left glove raised, the right hand cocked, head tucked behind his left shoulder, and McCloud said softly, "So you know how to box, kid."

Ron just nodded. He started circling toward his left,

shooting the left hand out gently as he did so.

"It won't do you too much good," Bo observed.

He was the slugger type, the man who drove in with both fists, hammering down the fighter in front of him, and he had his contempt for the fancy boxers.

"Get to it," Ron smiled, and then he jabbed McCloud gently on the nose.

Bo settled himself a little lower, shoulders hunched, in a half crouch. When he came in he moved very fast, ripping the punches up from the waist, hard, vicious shots, aimed at Ron's body.

Very easily Ron moved away from him. Bo missed with a right and Ron hooked him hard with a left to the head which made Bo's head bounce. Bo stared at him because there had been plenty of sting behind that punch.

Again Bo tore in but Ron side-stepped him, ducked under another wild swing, and then smashed McCloud hard in the ribs with the right. Bo McCloud pulled up, again surprised.

Ron moved in very fast now, jabbing with the left, putting more behind it, and then driving the right to the body. When Bo tried to retaliate Ron was moving away, dancing high, a very beautiful boxer with a real hard punch.

The Turbine players seemed stunned as Ron moved around confidently, jabbing Bo almost at will now, making him miss, feinting, and then shooting hard shots to the head and body. Bo on his part seemed unable to land a punch. He missed, lunged in wildly, and missed again, Ron either rolling away from the punches or taking them on his elbows.

The man was amazingly strong, though, and he kept boring in, always trying to land that big haymaker. Ron missed with a left hook and now McCloud caught him with a right as he was coming in. Ron's head bounced and McCloud hit him with a left to the head. Ron staggered now and sat down.

Breathing heavily, McCloud stood back, watching him.

"Had enough, kid?" he panted. His nose was puffed from Ron's jabs.

Ron got up without too much trouble, wiped the gloves off on his trunks, smiled and said, "Let's go, Bo."

McCloud tore in at him, thinking to finish the fight quickly and mercifully, but this time, instead of retreating, Ron moved in, smashing Bo hard in the body with a right hand, and then hitting him six times with rights and lefts, driving McCloud back.

A hard left to the head knocked Bo to the floor, and Rocco Sterovitch said in awe, "He's *down!* Bo's down!"

McCloud got up immediately, but Ron knocked him down again, this time with a swinging right to the jaw. McCloud got up more slowly, his eyes looking a little vacant. Ducking his head between his shoulders, he drove in courageously.

Ron jabbed at him with the left, stopping him, and then when Bo lifted his head, he feinted with the left and shot the right. He had the opening this time, a clear shot, and he did not miss. There was a sharp spat like a rock striking mud, and Bo McCloud dropped to his hands and knees. Then he rolled over on his side.

Quietly, Ron walked over to Stretch Moynihan and held up the gloves. He said, "You mind taking them off, Stretch?"

Moynihan looked at him and then at Bo McCloud on the gym floor and he said softly, "I don't mind at all, kid, not at all."

Rocco Sterovitch got a wet sponge from the locker room and wet Bo's face with it. Ron came over then and knelt down beside them. Rocco said,

"What a punch, kid! What a punch!"

Bo McCloud came around very quickly, eyes blinking as he looked at them. For a moment he looked at Ron stupidly as if trying to remember where he was and what had happened. He said slowly, "What happened, Rocco?"

"You been knocked out, Bo," Rocco explained solemnly. "This kid's a killer."

Bo McCloud sat on the floor, staring straight ahead of him. Then he rubbed his chin ruefully and looked up at Ron. "I don't believe it," he said. "I musta been tripped an' hit my head."

He was grinning as he spoke, though, and when Ron put out a hand to him to help him up, he grabbed it and came up off the floor.

"What a punch!" he said shaking his head. "Don't none

o' you guys work on him any more."

"We saw the fight," Moynihan told him. "From now on this kid says, 'Jump through a hoop,' we jump through a hoop."

Ron looked from one player to the other. They were all grinning at him and he saw the respect in their eyes. Rocco Sterovitch formed a kind of crown out of a white towel and placed it on Ron's head.

"Winner an' new champion," he said. "He could even lick *me!*"

Adam Greer called Ron on the phone that night back at the hotel and he said, "How was the practice session, Ron?"

"Went over all right," Ron told him.

"No trouble?"

Ron smiled. "Nothing that we couldn't work out," he said.

"Glad to hear it," Mr. Greer told him heartily. "I was a little worried. Let's look for a win against Pittsfield."

"We'll be trying," Ron said. "It's a good team, Mr. Greer."

It was a good team, a far better team than he'd ever expected to find here in the Willmantic Valley, and now they were all behind him. He'd gotten off to a good start.

6

Ron held another workout with the Turbines on the high-school court and then went down with them to Union Hall for the opener against the Pittsfield Ironmen, a team which Bennie Andrews had warned Ron was rough and tough, and which had nearly beaten out the Turbines for second place the previous year.

"Big team in this league," Bennie explained, "is the Allegheny Pipe Company Rockets. Studs Magruder of the Rockets has led the league in scoring for three straight years. They lick us every time out."

"We'll worry about the Ironmen first," Ron told him.

"One headache at a time," Bennie said with a grin.

As Ron had anticipated, Union Hall was jammed for this opening game. It was the same noisy, vociferous crowd he'd sat with when the Turbines had played the Wheelers in the exhibition game. This night every seat was taken and there were standees in the back. A four-piece band of Atlas Company employees had one corner of the hall jumping.

Bo McCloud trotted out on the floor first in his red Turbine jacket with the little figure of Atlas on his back.

The other players followed as the crowd roared, and Ron brought up the rear, knowing as he came out on the hardwood that these hard-bitten industrial league fans were watching him curiously.

The Ironmen had brought several busloads of rooters with them and they formed a noisy group in the balcony just above the Ironman bench. As Ron picked up a loose ball in the preliminary warm-up and tossed it toward the basket, an Ironman fan shouted, "Hey, McCloud, where'd you pick up sonny boy?"

There were more good-natured jibes from the Ironman contingent because Ron most certainly did look out of place with these rough industrial league players, all of whom were considerably older than himself.

A fan yelled to Bennie Andrews, "Hey, Bennie, you bring your *son* down tonight?" But Bennie just grinned and rubbed his semibald head.

Back in the dressing room before coming out on the court, when Ron had announced the starting line-up, he'd seen the surprise on some of the faces of the players. They'd assumed that he would be inserting himself with the regulars after what he'd shown in practice, but he'd decided that he'd start the first team of McCloud, Sterovitch, Moynihan, Mackey and Andrews, and fill in himself along with the four other utility men, Georgie Kramer, Doug Maceo, Chuck Abrams and Larry Sauer.

Moynihan had said privately, "You ain't startin' the game, kid?"

"I'll be in and out," Ron assured him. "We're using a lot of fast breaks and that means some of you fellows, especially Bennie, will have to come out for breathers."

Ron had noticed, already, that Andrews, even though surprisingly fast for a man of his build and age, couldn't keep it up for any length of time, and he'd resolved to give Bennie plenty of rest so that he could go at top speed whenever he was on the floor.

As usual some of the Atlas Power bigwigs were sitting in the seats beyond the Turbine bench. Ron saw Adam Greer there, along with several other very important-looking men. Millicent was sitting nearby, and she smiled and nodded to Ron as he walked toward the bench just before the teams took the floor. Adam Greer grinned, also, and lifted two fingers in the V-for-Victory salute.

In the huddle just before the team took the floor, Ron said, "Start moving it fast. We want to get the jump on this bunch."

When he walked back to the bench, his jacket still on, he thought he saw the disappointment in Millicent's eyes because he wasn't starting the game.

The Pittsfield Ironmen in blue and white uniforms were big and rugged, as Ron anticipated all these teams would be. They'd finished third in the league standings the year before, being beaten out by Atlas for second place. They had a 230-pound center who was as tall as Stretch Moynihan and yet seemed to be surprisingly fast on his feet.

Stretch got the tap on him, though, nudging the ball to Bennie Andrews who came in very fast. Bennie whipped it to Rocco Sterovitch, and the Turbines were moving downcourt, with the crowd yelling.

Moynihan slid into the bucket, took a pass from Bo, and fired it out to Sterovitch. Bennie Andrews went around a block set up by Jig Mackey and Rocco fed him a bounce pass on the run, Bennie netting the ball cleanly.

The Turbine crowd roared appreciatively, and Ron grinned. That set play had been one he'd worked with the team the second night of practice in the high-school gym.

The Ironmen came back fast, the big center, Joe Hoffman, moving into the slot and then throwing his weight back against Moynihan as the two tall men maneuvered for position close to the basket. Hoffman netted the ball a moment later on a hook shot as he elbowed Stretch out of the way.

Ron could see that Moynihan wasn't going to handle this big fellow the way he'd handled Abe Kindred of the Wheelers in the exhibition game. It could mean that they were in for a tough night.

Bo McCloud came back with a nice set shot from the corner and then Mackey went down the middle on a driving lay-up for another two-pointer, and the Turbines had a quick 6-2 lead.

The Ironmen came back with two free throws and a pair of field goals, one by the giant Hoffman, another hook, and they were in the lead. It was good, hard basketball, as rough and tough as it had been in the exhibition game Ron had seen, but he was a little more accustomed to it now.

With the score 19-15 for the Turbines after six minutes of play, Ron moved up to the scorer's table, waited for the horn, and then trotted out on the floor, nodding for Bennie Andrews to take a rest.

The Ironman crowd went to work on him without any waste of time.

"Hey, pretty boy," a rooter shouted from the balcony, "don't get that nice hair mussed up."

The Ironmen had the ball out of bounds on the opposite side of the court and Ron moved up toward his man, a big, barrel-chested fellow with red hair and freckles named Shannon. Ron held out his hand and Shannon shook it briefly, sizing him up as he did so.

Shannon moved away, then, Ron going with him, following him underneath the basket, letting him move out again, but even as he played Shannon he was watching Joe Hoffman shifting around in the bucket, leaning his weight back against Moynihan and waiting for that throw-in from outside.

When an Ironman player did bounce the ball in, Ron cut across very fast, breaking in on the pass. He whipped the stolen ball to McCloud and yelled, "Go!"

Jubilantly, Bo tore upcourt, moving the ball to Sterovitch who gave it to Jig Mackey cutting in from the side.

Mackey went up high with the shot, the ball, however, rolling off the rim.

Ron, coming on behind very fast, tapped it back in for the two-pointer. It was his first score in industrial league basketball and the Turbine crowd liked it.

Bo McCloud slapped Ron's back as they broke away from the basket.

A few moments later Shannon tried a quick break for the basket, taking a pass from outside, but Ron stayed with him, getting a hand on the ball as Shannon attempted the lay-up and deflecting it.

Stretch Moynihan picked up the loose ball and the Turbines were off again, the ball being whipped back and forth across the court.

Ron scored for the second time on a lay-up, going down the middle this time and taking the feed from Moynihan in the bucket. He had his half-step on Shannon and there was no chance for the redhead to block the shot. He went up high with Ron, however, trying to slap the ball away, and accidentally Ron took an elbow on the cheekbone which stunned him for the moment.

"Our boy!" Bo McCloud yelled at him.

The Turbines moved ahead gradually to a 36-31 lead, with Ron pulling Sterovitch out of the game for a breather, and then going out, himself. Playing with these men now he'd really begun to appreciate their skills. The regulars were all good floormen and ball handlers. Jig Mackey could thread the needle with his passes, while

McCloud and Sterovitch were able to move the ball with the best Ron had ever played against.

At half time it was 54-49 for the Turbines, a real, fast-moving game, and the Atlas crowd was tremendously pleased. Bo was high man at the half with sixteen points. Sterovitch had eleven and Mackey ten.

In the dressing room Ron said to Stretch, "How's it going with that Goliath out there?"

The tall center shook his head. "That big bum kills me," he said with a grin. "He's putting all his weight on me under the basket."

"I'll give you a breather now and then, next half," Ron said. "We'll put Rocco on him."

Jig Mackey said suddenly, "I'd put McCloud on Hoffman and let Rocco keep that other big fellow, Perkins. Rocco's scoring well against him."

Ron thought about that for a moment. "Makes sense," he agreed. Rocco was a considerably faster man than Perkins, and he had been scoring points tonight.

They came out for the third period, Ron starting himself with the regulars and keeping Bennie out for the time. After five minutes of play he took Moynihan out and put McCloud on big Hoffman. With Rocco Sterovitch still playing the slow-moving Perkins, Rocco continued to score points, which proved Jig Mackey's suggestion had been a good one.

In the fourth period it was 87-69 for the Turbines, who were moving the ball beautifully with Ron sparking the attack. The passing was smooth and fast, and some of the set plays Ron had introduced were producing results.

"This is a ball team," Rocco Sterovitch said exultantly. "Bring on them Rockets."

It was 103-89 for the Turbines when the gun went off and the team headed for the dressing room. The big Atlas crowd gave them an ovation as they left the court.

In the locker room Ron said quietly, "I'm really proud of this team. We were going great tonight."

"We got a real coach now," Stretch Moynihan said with a grin. "No reason why we shouldn't go places."

Ron passed Jig Mackey at his locker and he slapped Jig's back as he went by. "That was a good idea keeping Rocco on Perkins, Jig," he said. "It helped us tonight."

"Thanks." Mackey acknowledged the compliment, but he didn't smile.

Ron went on to have a word with Bo McCloud, and as he walked he was thinking that Mackey was the only one taking the victory calmly. But then, that was Jig's way. He was always poised and relaxed out on the court, knowing exactly what to do all the time and invariably making the right play. It was good to have a man of his caliber on the team.

Bo said, when Ron paused beside him, "We're goin' to the top this year, Ron. All the way. You just watch that Magruder, though, when we play the Rockets next week. He's not only good but he's dirty. He'll make it tough for you."

"I'll watch him," Ron promised, and he was almost anxious to stack up against Studs Magruder now, having heard so much about him. Could the Rocket ace be that good and that nasty as a player? Ron didn't know. The game tonight had been hard but clean. Maybe the Rockets didn't all play that way, but he'd find out.

7

Bright and early the next morning Ron took a bus out to Atlas for his first half day of work. He'd made arrangements with Mr. Greer to report mornings to the plant, working in the various departments and learning as much as he could about the giant power plant.

"It'll be a good apprenticeship for you," Adam Greer had told him. "I'm putting you in the boiler room for a week; in the pump room for another week. To begin with, though, I think we'll start you with the maintenance crew."

Ron reported to Paul Ormsby, the stocky, round-faced little engineer who'd accompanied him around the plant the first day.

"There's a maintenance crew heading up the valley in a few minutes," Mr. Ormsby told him. "I'll sign you on with them, Ron. McCloud and Moynihan are going out with the truck. They'll show you the ropes." He paused, shaking his head grimly. "We've been having insulator trouble. Somebody with a warped sense of humor is shooting insulators off the poles and knocking out the power here and there. Either that or it's a case of sabotage."

"Sabotage?" Ron repeated in surprise.

Ormsby shrugged. "Atlas Power supplies some very important companies with electrical current," he said. "It's not inconceivable, but I rather suspect juvenile delinquents, myself. We've notified the state police and the local sheriff, but it's a big valley with a good many hundred miles of power line. It's impossible to guard every mile of it."

Ron left, hurrying across the yard to the garage where the orange maintenance trucks were kept. A four-man crew was just preparing to roll when Ron arrived. Bo McCloud and Stretch Moynihan were in the back of the repair truck which was filled with all sorts of electrical repair gear, coils of rope, wire, setting poles, digging tools of all kinds.

"Going with you," Ron said with a grin as he jumped into the back of the truck.

Stretch said amiably, "You're on maintenance now, Ron. Welcome aboard."

Ron sat down on a coil of rope as the truck rolled out of the yard. Bo, sitting next to him, leaned back against a tool-box and said, "So you're starting at our end, Ron."

"That's it," Ron nodded. "I'll be on maintenance a week or so and then transfer indoors. Mr. Greer feels it's the best way for me to become acquainted with the plant." He paused and then said, "What about these insulators, Bo?"

Bo shook his head. "Happened three times the last week

or so," he explained. "Somebody's been sharpshooting at them with a rifle. It's no joke when you knock out that big atomic laboratory upriver, even for a few hours."

They rode a long way up the valley before they turned onto a twisting macadam road and the driver of the truck pulled up at the pole where the insulators holding the power lines had been smashed by rifle fire.

The four-man crew got busy immediately. Moynihan went up one pole and McCloud the next one farther down the road as Ron watched from the ground, ready to assist if he were needed.

The driver of the truck lit up a cigarette and said to Ron, "If it's kids doin' this, Mr. Starrett, they're in for it."

Ron nodded and walked up the road toward the pole where McCloud was working. He was halfway between the two poles when he noticed some bright shiny objects in the gravel nearby. Bending down he picked up two spent cartridge shells from a .22 rifle. He studied the shells thoughtfully for a few moments before dropping them into his jacket pocket.

The more he considered the matter the more it seemed that this was the work of teen-agers out on a lark. It wasn't too likely that saboteurs would operate in this manner. They could only hope to knock out power on a few isolated lines for a matter of hours at a time, until a repair truck was able to reach the trouble spot, and this would hardly make it worth their while, unless they had something big lined up for later.

With new insulators affixed to the poles, the repair crew headed back to Willmantic, Ron riding in the back of the truck again. On the way he said to Bo, "You know of any teen-age gangs operating in town?"

Bo scratched his chin. "Pretty rough crowd hangs out around the Lincoln Heights section," he said. "Guess every town the size of Willmantic has a gang or two, Ron. You figure some kids have been knockin' out these insulators?"

"If I were investigating," Ron smiled, "I'd begin with that assumption."

Then the thought suddenly struck him. Why not investigate? He had plenty of time in the afternoons, and this *was* company business. He could do Atlas a great service if he were able to apprehend the insulator shooters.

Back at the office he spoke to Mr. Ormsby about it, and the engineer accepted the plan readily.

"Whoever is shooting down the insulators," Ormsby said, "will be wary of the police or police patrol cars. You'd be able to circulate a lot easier than they."

"I'm picking up a used car this afternoon," Ron told him, "and I thought I'd do a little crusing in and around Willmantic. I understand that they usually hit within a few miles of town."

"That's right," Ormsby nodded. "If it is a gang of kids they probably come from Willmantic City. Good luck to you."

Before leaving the plant that afternoon Ron dropped

in to see Millicent Brown, and it was the first time he'd seen her since the Wheeler game.

"How did you like it?" he asked.

"The team has improved tremendously," Millicent said with enthusiasm. "I know enough about basketball to see that."

"It's a good team," Ron said sincerely.

"And you seem to get along with them," Millicent observed as she toyed with a pencil on her desk. "I thought you might be running into trouble, Ron."

"No trouble," Ron assured her. "They're a fine bunch."

"You really mean that, don't you?" Millicent said thoughtfully. "You're a college man; you're not being condescending?"

"I just like them," Ron replied, "and not only as basketball players."

He told her, then, about the detective work he was planning on doing for the next few days, and Millicent was immediately interested.

"I hope you catch them, Ron," she said, "whoever they are. I know Mr. Greer is quite worried. He's been getting complaints from some of the companies in the valley."

"I'm just going on a hunch," Ron explained, "and I may be all wrong. It's like looking for a needle in a haystack, but I may be lucky."

He visited several used car lots that afternoon on the outskirts of Willmantic and was able to make a deal for a three-year-old model which seemed to be in good condition.

He tried out the car on the highway for an hour or so and then drove back to town, ascertained the location of the Lincoln Heights section of Willmantic City, and headed in that direction.

Lincoln Heights contained a half-dozen blocks of run-down tenement houses, and was located at the north end of town. It seemed that every corner had a saloon or tavern. Because it was now late afternoon and school was out, there were plenty of children on the streets this November day. Here and there, as he drove slowly, Ron noticed groups of boys of high-school age shooting baskets at barrel hoops they'd nailed to power-line poles.

For the most part the boys were hard-faced young fellows in leather jackets. He drove up one street and then down another. As he slowed down before one particularly noisy group, waiting for them to step out of the way of his car, he noticed two boys in black jackets on the sidewalk off to his left. They were having an animated conversation, and suddenly one of the boys sighted an imaginary rifle up at the top of the pole to which the barrel hoop was nailed. He made a noise with his mouth as if shooting a gun and then both boys were convulsed with laughter.

Ron Starrett drove on, but he knew now that he'd located the particular gang for which he was looking. Pulling up a half-block away he turned off the motor and watched the gang in his rearview mirror.

He still had no proof, of course, and he could not go back to Paul Ormsby and tell him that he'd found the culprits because a boy had pointed an imaginary gun at the top of a pole. He needed proof; he had to catch them in the act.

The insulator shooting had taken place outside of town, usually at a distance of several miles, which meant that one of them had a car of some kind. Ron had to watch for that car the next time they went out.

He sat for nearly an hour until it was dusk and the boys playing basketball broke up, scattering for different homes. He drove off, himself, then, making note of the street.

The next afternoon he was back, parked on the same street, this time facing the improvised basketball court. He'd wisely pulled up about thirty yards away and he sat with a batch of papers in his lap, pretending he was going over them but at the same time watching the street.

By four o'clock in the afternoon the gang had started to congregate again and an impromptu game was going on. At four-thirty, the jalopy arrived.

Ron sat up in his own car. The jalopy was at least a dozen years old and the fellow driving it seemed a few years older than the other boys in the street. He was thin with a sallow complexion and lank black hair. He got out of the car, lit up a cigarette, and sat on the fender watching the game. Ron judged that he was at least eighteen.

After awhile, during a lull in the game, some of the boys gathered around the car. Then five of them laughingly piled inside. Ron reached forward and turned on the motor of his own car. As the jalopy pulled away from the curb he drove forward, also, keeping about a block behind.

They rolled through town, Ron occasionally letting another car get in between himself and the jalopy so as not to arouse suspicion.

They moved down the main street of Willmantic and out on to the highway running east and west. It was nearly five o'clock now and the jalopy had its lights on. With its right rear tail light out, Ron had no difficulty following it even in the fairly heavy traffic leaving town.

Two miles out of Willmantic the jalopy pulled off to the right on a smaller road. Ron slowed down, waited until the car had gone over a ridge nearby, and then made his turn, also. The new road was heading back toward town.

As he crossed the ridge he could see the jalopy's single red light up ahead of him. A mile or so down the road the light started to blink as the brake was applied. The boys were pulling off on one side of the road.

It was a lonely section of highway, no houses in sight on either side and with heavy woods beginning just beyond the cleared skirt of the road where the power-line poles had been placed.

The six boys still sat in the car as Ron drove by. They

had no reason to be suspicious of him, as he was driving an unmarked automobile, but they played it safe, letting him drive out of sight.

As Ron went by around a bend in the road he slowed down, turned off his car lights, and then made a quick U-turn so that he was now facing the direction in which he'd come. He sat in the car wondering whether he ought to wait until he heard some shooting or ride straight up and apprehend the boys. He'd already made a mental note of the license number of the car so that it would be an easy matter to trace it.

As he was hesitating, though, he saw the beam of a very powerful flashlight being directed at the top of one of the poles around the bend in the road. He hesitated no longer. Gunning the motor he shot the car forward, snapping on his lights again and flicking on the high beam.

As he whipped around the bend his headlights picked up the jalopy parked on the shoulder of the road. Five of the boys were standing near the car. One of them, the thin fellow with the lank black hair, was directing the flashlight at the insulator on top of the pole. A sixth boy had walked about thirty yards down the road and was in the act of lifting a rifle to his shoulder when Ron's car lights fell full upon him.

There was no traffic at the moment, and Ron, moving the car fast, cut across the macadam toward the parked jalopy. As he went up on the shoulder he heard one of the boys near the car yell, "Cops! Get out!"

The five boys scrambled back into the car as Ron came rolling down the gravel toward them, tires screeching. They'd apparently left the car running, and now as Ron pulled up alongside, the driver suddenly gunned the motor and shot away, leaving the boy with the rifle still standing where he was, staring after them.

Ron caught a glimpse of the driver's white, frightened face as he drove past, tires kicking up the gravel. Once on the road the jalopy picked up speed, shooting around the bend and disappearing.

The boy with the rifle still stood on the shoulder of the road some thirty yards from Ron, the car lights full upon him. He was a rather scrawny boy of about fifteen in a black leather jacket, hatless, his dark hair ruffled in the breeze.

Ron called to him sharply, "Stay where you are, fellow."

The boy with the rifle dropped it and cut for the thick woods to his right.

"Hold it!" Ron shouted as he jumped out and took after him.

On open ground Ron was positive he could have kept up without too much difficulty, but the boy in the black jacket had darted in among the trees out of the light from the car and it was going to be a problem keeping him in sight.

"Hold it!" Ron called again, but the boy kept going and Ron could hear him crashing through the underbrush up ahead.

Even though he realized it was quite foolhardy to run at this rate of speed through the dark woods, Ron kept after him, holding his hands up high to keep the branches and twigs out of his eyes.

He must have followed the boy about fifty yards in among the trees, chasing him more by sound than by sight, when he suddenly ran out into thin air. It was completely unexpected. One moment Ron's feet were on solid ground and the next he was treading air, falling as if into a pit. There were trees beyond and he'd just come out from among trees, but at this spot there was a hole of some kind.

Ron felt himself falling and there was absolutely nothing he could do to stop himself. Instinctively, with an athlete's reflexes, he let his body go limp, hoping to break the full force of the fall.

He hit on rough stones at least six feet below the spot where he'd taken off. There was a sharp pain in his right knee as he twisted it, and then he fell forward, hands extended, trying to roll with the fall, and his head struck something hard. The light exploded through his brain and he remembered nothing more.

8

After awhile Ron became conscious of something wet and cold being pressed against his forehead. Someone was saying in a rather frightened voice, "You all right now, mister? Are you all right?"

Ron opened his eyes. It was very dark where he lay, but far above he could see stars twinkling in the sky. His head was throbbing violently and he had to close his eyes for a few moments, waiting until the pain passed. When he opened them again, he looked up into the dim face of the person who was holding the cold compress to his forehead.

"You all right?" the boy was asking anxiously.

Ron remembered, then, that he'd been following one of the boys from the jalopy.

"Where are we?" he asked, his voice weak. "Who are you?"

"You were followin' me," the boy told him. "I—I was in that car. You fell into this old house foundation. I heard you cry out and—and I came back."

Ron sat up, his head still banging. "I'm obliged," he said. "You were the fellow with the rifle?"

"Yeah," the boy nodded. "I guess you got me, mister."

"You could have run off with the others," Ron told him thoughtfully.

"And leave you here in this hole?" the boy asked. "You coulda been dead!"

Ron felt of his head. There was no blood but he had a bad lump on one side of his skull.

"I must have struck a smooth stone down here," he observed. "I guess I was lucky, though."

"I was luckier," the boy told him with a short laugh. "I just missed it." He stood up now and he said, "I'll help you back to the car."

Ron stood up and it was then that he felt the pain in his right leg. He'd twisted the knee slightly when he fell and, while it wasn't so bad that it affected his walking, he knew it would be worse tomorrow.

They climbed out of the abandoned foundation, Ron still a trifle shaky but, by the time they reached the road, beginning to feel better.

"You gonna take me to the police?" the boy asked quietly.

Ron frowned, remembering that if it had not been for this boy he'd still be lying unconscious back in the woods.

"What's your name?" he asked.

"Johnny Baker," the boy said. "You a detective?"

"I work for Atlas Power," Ron told him. "We've been trying to catch you fellows for some time. It was a foolish thing to do, shoot down insulators."

Johnny Baker nodded and shrugged. He had a thin face and a mop of dark hair. "You know how it is," he muttered. "Tip Dolan had the car and the .22 rifle. We figured it was funny. You figure crazy things sometimes."

"Your pals pulled out on you," Ron observed.

"They got scared," Johnny told him. "They figured you were a detective in an unmarked car."

"We'll pick them up," Ron told him. "I have the car license number." He added, "That Dolan seems to be somewhat older than you fellows."

"He's eighteen," Johnny explained, "and he quit school years ago. I guess he's been in trouble with the police before."

"And it was his idea?" Ron asked.

Johnny frowned. "We went along," he admitted. "We're as much to blame."

"The other fellows still in high school?" Ron asked as they were getting into the car.

"We're in high school," Johnny nodded.

"And you have a lot of time on your hands," Ron mused. "How about sports? Aren't you fellows interested in sports? I noticed you were playing basketball in the street before you left with Dolan?"

"You were watchin' us?" Johnny asked, surprised.

"I've been keeping an eye on your gang," Ron stated.

"Well," Johnny told him, "some of us went out for basketball at Willmantic High but we didn't have the height. You're not over six feet these days, they don't even look at you, even in high school. We like to play, but what are we gonna do?"

"I see," Ron said. He realized that what Johnny Baker was telling him was the truth. All over the land the high-school and collegiate coaches were looking for the tall boys who could control the ball under the basket. Small and even average-sized fellows, unless they were exceptional, were scarcely considered. It meant that a great many boys never would have the opportunity of participating in an organized winter sport like basketball. With too much time on their hands, they were getting into trouble, aided by older delinquents like Tip Dolan. "So you like basketball?" Ron said again.

"Nuts about it," Johnny agreed. "We play in the street. We play anywhere we can."

"I like basketball, too," Ron told him. "As a matter of fact, I play it for Atlas Power."

Johnny Baker suddenly squirmed around on the seat. "No!" he ejaculated. "Hey! You're the new coach! I saw you against the Wheelers."

"I played my first game last week," Ron admitted.

"Boy, you're terrific," Johnny went on enthusiastically, "and the team's much better, too. Some of the other guys in our bunch saw that Wheeler game. Wait'll I tell them." He stopped suddenly, then. "Hey," he said softly, "we're in trouble, ain't we?"

"I'll have to turn you over to the police, of course," Ron told him, "and I'll give them the license number of

Dolan's car, but we'll see what we can do for you."

Already, his mind was moving rapidly. He, himself, had come from a small, orderly town with no juvenile delinquents in it, and no slum areas. He'd seen these boys shooting baskets in the street; he'd seen the kind of homes from which they'd come.

"Whatever happens to us," Johnny said slowly, "I guess we rate it, Mr. Starrett."

When they were back on the highway, Ron pulled up at the first phone booth he came to and called Adam Greer. He explained very briefly how he'd apprehended the insulator shooters and then he made a request.

"I'm taking one of the boys to the Willmantic police station, since this happened just within the city limits," he said. "Would it be possible for you to meet us there, Mr. Greer?"

"I'll be there," Mr. Greer told him over the phone. "Good work, Ron. Ormsby told me you were investigating this business."

Fifteen minutes later Ron was explaining what had happened to the police lieutenant at the desk when Adam Greer walked in.

The lieutenant, a young man with brown hair and a long jaw, frowned at Johnny Baker and said, "He's a minor and of course we can't hold him here. He'll go to the juvenile shelter and then for a hearing before the local judge if you intend to bring charges against him. We will, of course, pick up the older fellow."

Adam Greer said tersely, "It might teach some of these young toughs a lesson."

Ron explained to him, then, how Johnny Baker had come back to the cellar hole to help him out.

"I have an idea, Mr. Greer," he stated quietly, "and I'd like you and the lieutenant to listen to it before we take any action."

"Go ahead," Mr. Greer said.

"I'm working part time at the plant," Ron stated, "which means that I have my afternoons free. I want to organize a kind of junior basketball team to represent Atlas the way the Turbines represent the company to the public. We could call them the Kilowatt Kids or something like that and play in an amateur league. The uniforms wouldn't cost very much and I could do the coaching in the afternoons. Perhaps we could make arrangements to practice in some gym in town and work the Kilowatt Kids in as a pre-game attraction at our home games."

Johnny Baker was listening, open mouthed. "Boy!" he whispered. "Boy, oh, boy!"

Adam Greer looked at the lieutenant, who was nodding thoughtfully. "Sounds good to me, Ron," he said. "You'd be helping a bunch of boys who obviously need help, and you'd be advertising the company at the same time. I'll go along with it. If you start this team I think we can drop the charges against the younger boys." He turned, then, and he said to Johnny, "How about it, Baker? Can you round up your friends?"

"Can I?" Johnny whooped. "I can get them tonight if you want."

Ron said to Adam Greer, "I think this will work out, Mr. Greer."

"We need more of that kind of work in this town," the lieutenant said quietly. "Good luck to you, Starrett."

Ron drove Johnny Baker home, made arrangements to meet him and his friends the following afternoon in the neighborhood, and then went back to the hotel.

After he'd parked the car and walked the block to the hotel, he noticed that the knee was bothering him considerably, and tomorrow night they had to face the fast-moving Allegheny Rockets with the tough Studs Magruder in the line-up. Furthermore, Ron was scheduled to go against Magruder when he was playing, this on the advice of both Bennie Andrews and Bo McCloud.

"You're fast enough to hold him," Bo had said. "The guy's a streak. He doesn't know you, yet, and you might give him trouble."

"I'll play him when I'm in," Ron had said.

As he walked down the street now he kicked out with the right leg several times, wondering how bad it actually was. He could walk and he could run, and possibly by tomorrow night he could work the pain and stiffness out of it and be ready for Studs.

He didn't like to think of staying out of the game altogether. The Turbines needed him and he'd already agreed to work against Studs. If he kept himself out of the game now because of a slightly injured leg it just wouldn't look too good. They might think he was *afraid* to go against Magruder.

He'd played other games when he wasn't in top physical condition and he'd play this one. He did wish, rather wryly, though, that it was against another, less formidable opponent.

9

The Allegheny Pipe Company Rockets came out on the floor dressed in gaudy orange and black outfits, orange socks with black stripes, orange sweatsuits and black uniforms with orange piping.

Stretch Moynihan pointed out the Allegheny ace, Studs Magruder, as the team trotted out on the court.

"He's fast," big Stretch said to Ron, "and he's dirty. So you better watch him real close, kid." He added with a grin, "I'm glad I don't have him."

Magruder was just under six feet, a wiry, tawny-haired, thin-faced chap with cold blue eyes, a tough, jutting chin, and a twisted nose.

"Studs has been high scorer in this league the last few years," Bennie Andrews told Ron. "He can shoot and he can move the ball. He's the best floorman in the league."

Ron just nodded. The knee didn't feel too bad. He could run but he knew definitely that he wasn't in the best of shape. Again he thought of keeping himself out of this game altogether and letting Bennie Andrews and one of the utility men worry about Magruder, but he decided against it. It would look rather odd, his begging off suddenly when he wasn't even limping and when he was about to play against the top man in the league. Besides, the Atlas fans were looking for big things tonight, and they expected the new coach to provide the extra drive.

A large contingent of Rocket rooters had come down from the nearby town of Allegheny just outside the valley, and they were whooping it up noisily at the teams lined up for the tap.

At the jump Studs Magruder slid in very fast, beating Bennie Andrews to the ball. He whipped it across to a Rocket player and they were off. This was a smooth, hard-driving quintet out on the floor, and, watching them, Ron could see why they'd been winning so regularly the past few years. The ball handling was excellent and the orange and black team had plenty of power under the boards. Also, they had Studs Magruder, whom Ron Starrett knew could have been All-American in the collegiate ranks.

Studs moved like a streak of light, feinting, making his breaks, moving the ball beautifully every moment. In less than two minutes of play he'd scored six points on Bennie Andrews and Bennie's tongue was beginning to hang out.

Bo McCloud and Sterovitch scored, which helped, but Mackey missed two lay-ups which was unusual for him. After five minutes of play the Rockets had a 19-14 lead.

At a Turbine time out, Ron signaled for Georgie Kramer to go in for Mackey, and he went out on the court, himself, to replace Bennie Andrews.

Studs Magruder said to him as he came up, "So you're

the new college boy."

Ron just nodded.

The Rockets had the ball outside and they started moving it upcourt, Ron falling back with Studs, keeping close to him, remembering the man's speed on the breaks.

Studs handled the ball several times, always passing it outside again, and then quite suddenly he slowed down as he maneuvered just back of the free-throw line. Ron stayed behind him, waiting for him to make a break.

Magruder leaned backward and then to Ron's complete surprise and chagrin Studs came down with his left heel hard on Ron's left foot. Pivoting off the foot, Studs broke toward the basket.

The tears of pain in his eyes, Ron took after him but Studs had a half-step and it was sufficient. Taking a looping pass from a teammate in the backcourt, Studs went up high with the lay-up, scoring another two-pointer.

Neither of the referees, nor any of the Turbine players, had seen Magruder's deft maneuver but Ron Starrett still felt the results of it as he started upcourt with the Turbines moving the ball.

This was something new to him. Even in this league he'd noticed that while the play was very rough, much rougher than any collegiate game he'd ever seen, these industrial league players for the most part played it clean. Obviously, Studs Magruder was the big exception. The other Turbine players had warned Ron what to expect from the fast-moving Rocket star and now he'd had a sample.

There was a lot more to come. Moving on his weak leg, and with the left foot hurting considerably from Magruder's vicious stomp, Ron did the best he could. He took a pass from Sterovitch and fired it out to Georgie Kramer. Bo McCloud bounced it in to Ron and he fed it to Moynihan in the bucket.

Ron noticed as he moved around with Magruder guarding him closely that he was constantly being pushed from the rear, or that a hand would clutch at his jersey for a brief second when he was about to break for the basket, making it extremely difficult to play a normal game of basketball. Studs did it so cleverly that, even though Ron realized the referees knew about his underhanded tactics, they could not catch him at it. With the ball moving around in the backcourt it was difficult watching every player under the basket. Besides, the industrial league referees were not accustomed to blowing the whistle every time a player was pushed or shoved.

As a result Ron found himself constantly off balance. It was the most exasperating basketball he'd ever played in his life, and there was very little he could do about it unless he wanted to retaliate.

Once the referee did call a holding foul on Magruder when he grabbed Ron's jersey. The single point Ron scored on the free throw, however, did not make up for the other things.

The knee wasn't getting any better, either. After five

minutes he'd scored only the one point on the free throw. He put Mackey back into the game, taking the bench, himself.

The Turbine crowd had become rather silent now, as the Rockets led by a 31-20 score. This team did not look at all like the quintet which had upset the Ironmen the previous week.

Mackey was very fast on the floor but he, too, had a difficult time keeping up with Studs Magruder, who seemed to be having one of his great nights. It wasn't only the defense which was weak for the Turbines tonight. Even when they had the ball they couldn't seem to get anywhere. A bounce pass ended up in the hands of a Rocket player. Then Jig Mackey, taking a pass from McCloud and out in the open this time, mishandled the throw and Magruder took it away from him.

All the way it was sloppy basketball, even though Bo McCloud, Sterovitch and Moynihan tried desperately to make it a contest. At half-time it was 58-40 for the Rockets, an eighteen-point spread, as the disconsolate Turbine team left the floor.

Rocco walked with Ron down the corridor to the dressing room and he said, "That bum, Magruder hurt your foot, Ron? I saw him step on it back there. You don't seem to have any drive tonight."

"It's not too bad," Ron admitted. The foot was all right now, but the knee was beginning to bother him. He knew that if he played very much the second half he wouldn't be an asset to the team.

After the inspiring start against the Ironmen it was very disappointing for the Turbines to have the Rockets rolling over them again as they'd done in previous years.

"We have to get that ball moving," Ron said in the dressing room. "The passing hasn't been too sharp tonight, and we must watch the shooting."

The Rockets had not been a one-man team by any means. They had big, fast men on the floor, men who could fight for the ball off the boards, and they, too, were giving Moynihan and Sterovitch a rough time of it. Magruder made the big difference, however. He had twenty-two points for the first half.

"Everybody on that ball the next half," Bo said grimly. "We can't let this bunch run us off the court."

When the team came back on the floor there were a few scattered boos from the disgruntled Atlas crowd, and listening to the boos Ron realized that, just as the town could root for its team, it could also turn against them just as easily. This, too, was different from collegiate basketball where the undergraduates stood by the team in fair weather or in foul.

The five regulars started the second half and they did fairly well in the first few minutes of it. Bennie Andrews, rested up, stayed with Magruder and the Turbines held the Rockets fairly even for six minutes, even though they could not start an offense of their own. For one reason or another the ball handling was still sloppy. Constantly, the Turbines seemed to be losing possession because of a pass which barely missed the outstretched fingers of a player.

Bennie broke around a stationary block and was cutting for the basket when Mackey fed him the ball. If Bennie had caught the pass it would have been a sure two-pointer, but the ball just grazed his fingers and went out of bounds.

When little Bennie started to tire, Ron sent in Doug Maceo and when Doug came out on the court a Turbine fan yelled from the rear, "What's the matter, Starrett? Don't you like playin' against Studs?"

Ron sat on the bench, red faced, looking down at the floor. He wasn't afraid of Magruder and he was confident that in good condition he could hold the Rocket ace in check fairly well, but not tonight, never tonight. He knew now what the Turbine fans were beginning to think. The previous week he'd played topnotch basketball, sparking the Turbines to a big win, but in the first half tonight he'd been outplayed and outscored by Studs Magruder. Now he seemed to prefer remaining on the bench rather than having Studs show him up. It was not a very pleasant picture of the new coach.

He went into the game in the fourth period, this time replacing Bo McCloud who obviously needed a break. The Rockets led 82-68. Very foolishly Ron took on Studs Magruder as his man. He could have made a switch and let Sterovitch or Mackey take Magruder, but he knew that if he did so the basketball-wise Turbine crowd would lose their respect for him completely.

With the knee really bothering him now, Ron tried to keep Studs in sight, but it was a hopeless task. Magruder feinted and broke for the basket; Magruder cut in around a block; Magruder shoved and took off as Ron desperately strove to stay with him. Studs scored and scored again, the Rocket total mounting as the Turbine crowd started to boo.

Ron scored once from the outside with a set shot and it was the only two-pointer he made in the entire game. With the score 108-82 for the Rockets, he took himself out in the final few minutes, putting in Larry Sauer.

As he walked toward the bench, picking up a towel, he glanced toward the seats where Adam Greer was sitting with Millicent Brown. He saw the disappointment in the superintendent's face. He remembered that it wasn't absolutely necessary for an industrial league team to be a winner, but the Turbines represented Atlas Power to the public and the employees wanted to be proud of their quintet. No one was ever proud of a loser!

The Turbines lost this one to the Allegheny Rockets by a 118-91 score with Studs Magruder high man with forty-three points. It was a discouraged Turbine team which trooped into the dressing room after the final whistle.

Rocco said, "We'll do better against the Wyoming Cowboys, Ron. Don't worry about it." He looked at Ron curiously and he added, "You sure that foot wasn't botherin' you, kid? You didn't have any drive out there."

"One of those bad nights," Ron told him. He added quietly, "I wasn't afraid to play Studs, Rocco."

He knew he couldn't tell these men now about the weak knee, because if it had been that weak he should have kept himself out of the game. It would only look as if he were making an alibi because he, the collegiate all-star, had been outclassed by an industrial league player.

Stretch Moynihan was saying glumly, "I don't know. It seemed like everything was goin' wrong tonight. Nobody had it."

Little Bennie said, the perspiration streaming down his fact, "That Magruder!"

Bo McCloud said tersely, "The next time I'd like to play that bum, myself, Ron, an' give him back some of his dirty work."

"The next time," Ron tried to smile, "I'll know what to expect."

He'd made arrangements to meet Millicent Brown after the game and have a bite to eat with her. As usual before a contest Ron had had a light supper and liked to stop in for a snack after playing.

Millicent said now, as she sat across from him in a little restaurant in town, "It was too bad about tonight, Ron. I wish, though, that our fans wouldn't boo when things don't go right."

Ron shook his head. "They were disappointed after

last week," he observed. "We really were way off."

"What happened?" Millicent asked curiously. "The team didn't seem to have too much drive."

Ron wondered if he ought to tell her about his leg because that, he felt, more than anything else, had accounted for the debacle. He decided against it, though. Again it would look as if he were coming up with an excuse for his poor showing against Magruder. He hadn't complained about a bad knee before and it was too late now.

"For one thing," he said slowly, "I didn't play much of a game tonight, and I was up against the best man in the league. That made a lot of difference."

"It wasn't just you, though," Millicent told him. "The team didn't look very good when you *weren't* playing, and you were on the bench quite a lot."

Ron had to concede that. The Turbines hadn't been very sharp all night, and he couldn't quite put his finger on why. They'd been "up" for the Wheeler game, and "down" for this one. It had been one of those bad nights when everything went wrong, when the passes were going awry.

"Well," he said thoughtfully, "we'll do better the next time out. I'm sure of that, Millicent."

He was thinking that they had to. He'd come here as basketball coach. What if his team were worse this year than it had been the previous year without a regular coach? It was something to think about.

10

Ron held his first practice session the following afternoon at four o'clock with his newly organized Kilowatt Kids. He'd already met with Johnny Baker and eight other boys from the Lincoln Heights section of town, all of whom were anxious to play basketball, and he'd made arrangements to work out in a grade-school gym which wasn't being used. He'd also investigated and discovered that there was an amateur league in the Willmantic Valley for boys of this age consisting mostly of church teams, and he'd enrolled his Kilowatt Kids in this league.

He still didn't know how well his team would play in competition, but even this was not of paramount importance. He was getting the boys off the street, involved in a sport, and that was enough for now.

When the nine boys got into the uniforms they'd dug up from various sources and began to move the ball around, though, Ron was agreeably surprised. Most of the boys were too small and not experienced enough to make the Willmantic High squad, but they were fast and what they lacked in ability they made up in drive and determination.

Johnny Baker said confidently, "We're gonna have a good team, Mr. Starrett."

"I'm sure of it," Ron nodded.

"You show us how," Johnny told him. "Teach us some of those plays."

"The plays didn't work too well against the Rockets," Ron said ruefully. "Did you see the game, Johnny?"

"I saw it," Johnny nodded. "That Studs played you dirty, Mr. Starrett. The next time you give him back everything he gave you."

Ron said quietly, "I'm playing *him* clean, Johnny, no matter how he plays me."

Johnny Baker stared at him. "That's nuts!" he said. "Studs *expects* it, Mr. Starrett!"

Ron shook his head. "Basketball's not a dirty game, Johnny," he pointed out. "Just because a few players in our league operate that way is no reason why the rest of us should follow suit. If everybody played it dirty you wouldn't have much of a game. It would be a free-for-all."

Johnny thought about this. "I don't know," he confessed. "Maybe you're right, Mr. Starrett, but I wouldn't like to take that pushin' around from Studs."

"I didn't like to take it, either," Ron admitted, "but I'm not going to make a boxing match out of a basketball game."

"You—you're not *afraid* of him?" Johnny asked hesitantly.

"No," Ron said soberly, "I'm not afraid of him, Johnny."

They had a scrimmage game and Ron played with one of the sides. His knee was considerably better this evening and he was sure the stiffness would wear off in a few more days.

For two hours the Kilowatt Kids worked out on the school floor with Ron teaching them how to move the ball sharply and cleanly.

"Try to work it to a man coming toward you," he said, "and don't forget that a bounce pass is just as good as any other kind. It's even easier to handle as a matter of fact. But whatever you do, don't throw the ball away. Keep possession as long as you can, and when you do attempt your shots, make them good. More games are lost by wasted shots than anything else."

"You hear that?" Johnny Baker said. "No crazy shootin'. The first guy starts throwin' it wild has to talk to me."

"Well," Ron smiled, "we won't do it that way, but try to hang on to that ball. If you don't have a clear shot, pass off."

He showed them a few simple set plays and pick-offs, and before the session was over the boys were highly enthused.

"When is our first game?" Johnny Baker wanted to know. "We gotta work this stuff on somebody else."

"We open against Christ Church on Thursday night," Ron said.

"Church guys!" Johnny chuckled. "We oughta murder them."

"Maybe you won't," Ron warned. "Some of these church teams have been playing together for a long time. And remember, no dirty stuff. The first man on this squad who gets rough is out of the game. And you do it too often and you're off the squad. Is that clear?"

The nine boys stared at him and then Lou Carino, a short, dark-haired fellow, said, "I think it's clear, Mr. Starrett. You want to make gentlemen out of us."

"Just *men,*" Ron said. "That's good enough for me."

There were three more recruits for the Kilowatt Kids when the team took the floor against the Christ Church quintet several days later. Millicent Brown had managed to put through a hurried order for uniforms and they arrived just before the game.

When Ron opened the boxes in the Christ Church dressing room the boys stared and then let out whoops of joy. The uniforms Millicent had designed were white with purple trim. They had the Atlas insignia on the jackets with the words "Kilowatt Kids" beneath.

"Boy! They're knockouts!" Johnny Baker said.

"Let's start off with a win tonight," Ron told them. "We've only had two practice sessions but you've been going good. Don't forget what I told you about 'possession' basketball. Don't throw it away."

"The first guy throws it away—" Bud Holloway started to say, and then he stopped and grinned. "Aw, you know what I mean," he finished lamely.

Ron sat on the bench as the Kids took the floor against a good Christ Church squad. The Atlas boys started off with a bang, scoring three quick baskets, and the substitutes on the bench were whooping it up happily.

Christ Church came back, though, and gradually pulled ahead. They were a more experienced team, somewhat better ball handlers and better shooters. At the end of the first period it was 18-12 for the church team, and Ron could see that his Kilowatt Kids didn't like it.

Johnny Baker's man was high scorer, a very fast, dark-haired fellow with quick hands. As the Christ Church boy started to pile up the points, Johnny's face grew tight. Twice he roughed his man on the way up to the basket and the referee called fouls on him. The third time it happened, Ron pulled him out of the game.

"That lucky bum!" Johnny panted as he came in and sat down near Ron.

"He's not lucky," Ron said quietly. "He's a better man than you, Baker, and in more ways than one. I don't think he'd be playing you dirty if you were scoring the baskets."

"Who played him dirty?" Johnny asked with pretended innocence.

"*You* did," Ron said flatly, "and if you do it again when you go back in you're out for the remainder of the game. Remember that."

Crestfallen, Johnny sat on the bench until the half was up. In the locker room he said pleadingly, "Let me get in there again, Mr. Starrett. I'll watch it this time."

The score was 28-23 at half time, and starting the third period Ron put Johnny Baker back into the game.

"Remember, Johnny," he said, "anybody can play it clean when he's winning. It takes a man to keep his temper when he's losing."

Johnny Baker went out on the court again, and this time, even though the Christ Church boy continued to score, Johnny did the best he could without the rough tactics.

After the game, which was won by Christ Church with a 47-39 score, Johnny said quietly, "That was the hardest game I ever played, Mr. Starrett."

"I know it," Ron told him, "and you *won* it."

"We didn't win!" Johnny said, surprised. "They licked us."

"You won," Ron smiled. "They only licked you with the score." He paused, and then added, "You'll be doing much better in the future. I think the team did surprisingly well for a new squad like this. Wait'll we've had a few weeks of practice. Everybody out on the school gym tomorrow afternoon at four o'clock sharp. O.K.?"

"We'll be there," Bud Holloway told him.

Ron looked at the sweaty-faced boys in the dressing room, seeing the enthusiasm in their eyes, and he was thinking that this was the secret: keep them busy, keep them off the streets, have them doing things they like to do—and there was nothing they liked better than sports.

"You see that big center hook me on that last shot I tried?" Bud Holloway asked. "I was all set to lay him out an' then I remembered I'd be out myself. I thought, I better not."

"By the end of the season you'll be outplaying that fellow," Ron told him. "You won't need to lay him out, Bud."

"Sure," Bud said with a grin. "There's more than one way to skin a cat."

Lou Carino said almost in awe, "We played the whole game an' not a fight! How do you like that?"

"We can play every game without a fight," Ron told him.

Millicent had come down to watch this opening game of the Kilowatt Kids and she was waiting for Ron outside.

"They did quite well, didn't they, Ron?" she asked when he came up.

"A lot better even than they know," Ron said softly. "They were not only battling the other team tonight but *themselves,* also, and I think they won."

"It's a good start, Ron," Millicent told him. "I think it's a wonderful work and I'm glad you started it."

"They're a lot better off here than in a juvenile court or a reform school," Ron said. "And you did a wonderful job with the uniforms. The boys are crazy about them."

"A little gaudy," Millicent said with a grin, "but I thought they'd like that better."

"They're good boys," Ron observed. "They've come

from rather rough backgrounds but they'll turn out all right."

"As long as somebody works with them," Millicent added. "Somebody by the name of Ron Starrett. Whether you know it or not, Ron, you are now a social worker in addition to being an electrical engineer and a basketball coach!"

The Kilowatt Kids played another game two nights later and this time to their great joy they won by a narrow 53-52 margin. It was Johnny Baker who scored the winning shot in the final seconds, going in with a lay-up.

The game had been quite cleanly played all the way with only one little skirmish marring it. It was the quiet little Lou Carino this time who was goaded into using his fists by a boy from the opposing Liberty A.C. Both boys were ejected from the game, and Ron said to Lou when he came off the floor, "That was a tough one, Lou. He *was* working you over."

"The next time," Lou said, *"he* goes out alone. If he really wants any rough stuff he can find me after the game."

"Play it clean," Ron told him. "They only hurt themselves when they get rough."

He was thinking as he said it that some of the industrial league players would be a lot better off if they also played with that thought in mind! It was a rough league, though, and these were grown men to whom the turn-the-other-cheek policy was quite alien.

His Kilowatt Kids team had gotten off to a wonderful start, win or lose, and he was tremendously pleased with the project. They would take a lot of handling in the next weeks and months but he was positive they would develop not only as basketball players but as *people*. And this was infinitely more important.

11

The Turbines took on the Wyoming Brass Company Cowboys the following night, traveling up to Bowdin in the Wyoming Valley. Ron's knee now seemed to be back to normal and he anticipated a good night.

The team drove up in three cars with several busloads of Turbine rooters coming after them, hoping to cheer Atlas back to its winning ways. The Cowboys from Wyoming Brass were fast, a relatively small team compared to some of the bigger outfits, but they could move the ball.

The Cowboys came running out on the floor in big white Stetsons, the brain child of some misguided public relations man. They discarded the sombreros which the players had worn rather sheepishly and then started to warm up. Watching them Ron realized that his Turbines would have to extend themselves if they wanted to pull this one out of the bag. The Cowboys could move and they were ably coached by an ex-high-school coach who knew his business.

Ron started the regulars, hoping that tonight they would show the kind of form they'd shown against the Ironmen, but again things started to go wrong.

The Cowboys broke fast, bringing the ball upcourt, employing good screens to set up their men, and when they shot they scored. On the other hand when the Turbines had possession something always seemed to be going wrong. A basket was missed, a pass bounced off someone's hand or was too high, and the Cowboys came roaring back again, playing possession basketball, hanging on to the ball until they scored.

With the Cowboys leading 23-14, Ron went into the game, replacing Andrews. Rocco said, when Ron came out on the court, "Let's get 'em movin' now, Ron."

Rocco looked worried, too, and Stretch Moynihan was shaking his head as if in disgust at something he didn't quite understand. The Turbines had the ball under their own basket and started upcourt, Ron taking the pass from Sterovitch, moving it over to Jig Mackey. Mackey bounced the ball in to Moynihan and Stretch whipped it back to McCloud.

Ron cut underneath the basket, faked his man out of position, and then broke back toward the rim. Mackey's pass from outside just grazed his fingers. The ball went out of bounds and the Cowboys took over.

That seemed to be the pattern of the game all evening as the disgruntled Turbine rooters, who had traveled a good distance to see the home town favorites, watched glumly. The Turbines never seemed to be able to sustain a steady drive. They would score a basket or two, and then a misplay, or a missed shot, would give the Cowboys the initiative again.

At half time it was 53-45 for the Cowboys, a better game than the Turbines had played against the Rockets but by no means satisfactory. Ron had seven points for the first half. McCloud was high man with eleven.

The team was very quiet in the dressing room. Ron said to them, "We'll snap out of this. We have to start moving that ball again. Keep the passes shorter. We're throwing the ball away too much."

They did better in the second half, creeping up on the Cowboys, tying them as they moved into the fourth period. Ron, still in for Benny, had worked the stiffness out of his knee by now and was going at top speed, sparking the new Turbine drive.

He scored on a lay-up, taking the bounce pass from Sterovitch. McCloud went down the middle on another driving lay-up, and they were two points ahead of the Cowboys.

Jig Mackey's hard pass got away from Stretch Moynihan in the bucket and an alert Cowboy picked it up and sped downcourt, passing to a teammate who promptly tied up the score again.

Because the team had been moving at top speed, and was beginning to feel it, Ron took Mackey and Moynihan out of the game, putting in Kramer at center and Larry Sauer for Mackey, and for a while the Turbines looked better with the two fresh men on the court, building up a six-point lead with five minutes to go. The Turbine crowd started to come alive.

Those final five minutes, though, with all the regulars back on the floor, the spark seemed to die out. Six points mean very little in a free-wheeling game and the Cowboys tied it up at 93-all with two minutes remaining.

Ron went back in, replacing Bennie who seemed to have had enough for the evening. Ron had a good opportunity to put the Turbines ahead as he broke free of his man and took Rocco's pass in under the basket. His lay-up rolled off the rim, however, and the Cowboys took the rebound.

A Cowboy tore in toward the basket with Mackey on top of him. As the Cowboy went up toward the rim Jig hacked him. The ball dropped through the net for a two-pointer and the Cowboy made good on the extra free throw. The three-pointer gave the Cowboys the game even though Mackey came through with a long set-shot in the final seconds of play which brought them to within one point of the winning score.

The Atlas team walked off the court with Rocco Sterovitch literally talking to himself.

"We shoulda won it, at least nine different ways," the Turbine player growled.

"My fault," Stretch said glumly. "I shoulda picked up half-dozen more points on my hooks. I sure was missin' them tonight."

It wasn't Moynihan, Ron knew, and tonight he'd played good basketball, himself, but they'd still lost. It was very discouraging.

In the morning a local sportswriter who had covered the Cowboy game claimed that the difficulties of the Turbines could be attributed to the new set plays, pick-offs and general system now employed by the young collegiate coach.

"The Turbines seemed to be a more alert team last year," the writer stated. "Perhaps young Starrett's coaching techniques do not quite apply to industrial league basketball."

Ron read the paper as he ate his breakfast in a restaurant in town. He had a feeling of doubt, himself. Was it possible that these set plays he'd taught the team were *not* what the Turbines needed? Maybe this type of basketball player got along better with the old-fashioned slam-bang game used previously.

Unlike the collegiate squads, these industrial league men all held down full-time jobs and couldn't be asked to practice for hours every evening as the collegians did to perfect the plays, and the set plays did need plenty of practice to smooth out the wrinkles.

Originally, Ron had hoped to work with the team once or twice a week, but now, with the schedule a lot stiffer than he'd anticipated and games coming up every few days, he didn't think this was advisable. Men like Moynihan and McCloud, climbing power-line poles, putting in a good hard day's work, could not be expected to practice and then have anything left for the actual game.

Reaching the plant, Ron stopped in at the control room where Bennie Andrews worked. He'd been in the control room before and Bennie had gone over the panels, explaining what each button, switch or knob meant. Ron said as he sat down at the desk across from the little Turbine player, "You read the article in the *Willmantic Blade* this morning, Bennie?"

"About the team?" Bennie asked. "I read it."

"What do you think?" Ron wanted to know. "You've been with the team longer than anyone else, Bennie. You think this new type of game I've introduced is hurting us?"

"No," Bennie said promptly. "It's good, Ron. All the other fellows think so, too."

"But we're losing," Ron reminded him.

Bennie shook his head. "I still think it's good," he said. "Those set plays are all right."

"Why are we losing then?" Ron persisted.

Bennie thought about it a moment. "The cause of it is sloppy ball handling," he said quietly. "That's the only way I can figure it out, Ron. We're not holding on to the ball long enough to score, and we miss shots we shouldn't miss. It doesn't take much to lose a basketball game, not when it's decided by two or three points. You miss a lay-up here; your man gets away on a break for the basket; a pass is thrown too hard or too soft. That's all it takes in a tight game. That Cowboy game could have been decided last night by one pass thrown away."

Ron nodded. "The Cowboys beat us by one point," he said. "I missed a lay-up I should have made. That alone would have given us the game."

"That's the way it is," Bennie agreed.

Ron stood up. He said quietly, "I'm new at this industrial league game, Bennie, and I'm new at coaching. I'm a lot younger than you fellows. If I'm doing things wrong I don't mind being told. I'll listen if you have any suggestions to make."

Bennie Andrews frowned and then looked at him steadily. "We like your style of basketball, Ron," he said. "I wouldn't change anything. I think we'll start to pick up soon."

"Thanks," Ron said gratefully, and he turned to go.

"Just one thing," Bennie called after him.

"What's that?" Ron asked.

Bennie sat at his desk looking down at the glass top. He hesitated a moment and then said, "I'd watch Jig Mackey if I were you."

Ron stared at the balding little man in amazement. "Mackey?" he repeated. "Jig?"

"Just watch him," Bennie advised. "That's all I'm going to say about it, Ron."

"You—you mean he's not going all out?" Ron asked, still bewildered.

"I'm not saying anything," Bennie said, "except that you should watch him."

Ron left the office, puzzled. It just didn't seem to make

sense. Why would Mackey play it loose? Was he taking gamblers' money? Ron was positive that there was some gambling going on in a league like this. Had Jig been "reached"?

He couldn't imagine what other motive Jig would have for not going all out. Perhaps Bennie had been mistaken. He, himself, hadn't noticed anything unusual about Jig's play. Jig had been one of the high scorers, and his exceptional passing in these opening games had often sparked the Turbine attack.

Ron told himself, though, that he would have to keep an eye on Jig during the next game or two just to make sure. It wasn't an assignment he liked, but as coach of the team he had to learn if Mackey was dogging it.

The Kilowatt Kids had a game that evening, and Ron drove Millicent to the church-basement court on the outskirts of Willmantic City, the rest of the team coming in two cars driven by fathers of the boys.

Ron noticed that since he'd started the basketball team some of the fathers were beginning to show a belated interest in their sons, and this was a good sign, too.

"It's a tough one tonight," Ron said to Millicent as he left her in one of the seats off the court. "We're playing the top team in our league."

"Good luck," Millicent said with a smile. "I'm rooting for the visiting team."

Johnny Baker said as they were getting into uniform, "Gosh, Mr. Starrett, what's happenin' to the Turbines?

I saw that Cowboy game. I thought you'd beat them easy."

"You can't win them all," Ron told him.

"The team just didn't look so hot," Johnny said, shaking his head. "Why, that first game against the Wheelers, I thought you guys were gonna win the championship this year."

Ron didn't say anthing to that. "Just think about tonight, Johnny," he stated. "You're going up against a really fine team, I understand."

The Kilowatt Kids got off to a flying start against the Church of the Messiah, Bud Holloway, Carino and the diminutive Tippy O'Day, smallest boy on the squad, leading the attack.

The Church team stormed back, though, in the second period, to catch up and pass the Kilowatt Kids. It was a hard-fought battle all the way, with plenty of body contact under the baskets as they battled for the ball. Ron waited for the trouble, supposing any moment that one of his Kids would start swinging.

Bud Holloway had taken an elbow in the lip and it was puffed badly. Johnny Baker had been sent flying into the seats on one occasion, even though the boy playing him had been on the ball and it had been clean.

At half-time it was Church of the Messiah 31, the Kilowatt Kids 29, with Baker high scorer.

Ron said between halves, "It's a rough one, but these fellows are playing it clean. Keep it that way."

The Kids did, all the way to the finish. They passed the

church quintet with less than three minutes remaining, but lost the lead in the final minute. Even in those last seconds, with Church of the Messiah freezing the ball, the Kids didn't lose their heads. They battled desperately to get possession but they kept it clean.

When the whistle blew, ending the game with Church of the Messiah the winner, Ron was proud of his team.

"Lost another one," Bud Holloway said glumly in the dressing room. "We just can't seem to win for you, Mr. Starrett."

"We're going good," Ron assured him. "I have no complaints."

"Those set plays sure were workin' good tonight, though, weren't they?" Lou Carino asked. "We almost had 'em."

"We'll take them the next time around," Ron told him. "These other teams in the league are beginning to worry about us, now."

"We're gonna keep them worryin', too," Johnny Baker vowed.

Before Ron left the team that night, Johnny said to him seriously, "Mr. Starrett, see if you can get the Turbines back on top the next time out, will you? We both play for Atlas now and we want a winner with the senior team, too."

"Don't worry about it," Ron said. "The Turbines are bound to come out of the slump pretty soon."

"Well," Johnny said, looking down at the floor, "we—

we just don't like that booin' they give you, Mr. Starrett. It ain't right."

"The booing will stop when we start to win," Ron told him. "I do appreciate your concern, Johnny."

On the way home with Millicent that night, when Ron had told her about Johnny's statement, she said simply, "They like you, Ron. They don't want to see you hurt."

"I haven't been hurt, yet." Ron smiled, but even as he said it he was thinking that things weren't going too well as far as the coach of the Atlas Turbines was concerned. He'd been brought here by Adam Greer first as a basketball coach, and secondly as an employee of the company. If he failed as coach and lost the support of the Atlas people who backed up these games, it was understandable that he would not make a very valuable Atlas man, himself. It was something to think about and, thinking about it, Ron Starrett was not particularly happy.

12

The Turbines played the Harrisburg Box Company Boxers the next night at Union Hall, and there were some boos when Ron came out on the court. A great many people had read the article by the Willmantic sports writer and they were now questioning the wisdom of bringing in an ex-collegiate as coach of the team.

The Boxers had finished in fourth place in the league standings the years before, but were said to be a tremendously improved team now. They were big, strong, a team that liked to storm the basket.

Ron sat on the bench at the opening tap, watching carefully. Bennie Andrews had told him to keep an eye on Jig Mackey and he intended to do that, even though he was quite sure Bennie was barking up the wrong tree. More and more Ron was coming to the conclusion that it was his coaching, his use of the new set plays, which had upset the Atlas applecart. There was no reason at all why Mackey, a solid Atlas employee, would want to see the Turbines lose.

Stretch Moynihan lost the tap and the Boxers took the ball, starting upcourt with it. The action was fast because the Harrisburg team was an aggressive outfit, keeping the ball on the move all the time.

First blood, however, was scored by the Turbines, Jig Mackey picking up a rebound and netting the ball nicely for two points. A short while later Mackey fired the ball down the middle to Rocco Sterovitch, a beautiful needle pass, and Rocco made the lay-up for another two points.

Ron squirmed on the bench, and he found himself wondering why Bennie had particularly picked on Jig Mackey as the man who might have been the cause of the team's slump. Jig *was* the best ball handler on the squad, superior even to Bo McCloud.

The Boxers came back quickly, tying up the score, and then Stretch Moynihan and Andrews hit twice in succession and the Turbines moved ahead. In the second period, with the score 31-28 for the Turbines, Ron came into the game with Doug Maceo. Bennie Andrews and McCloud went out.

Ron was in good shape tonight, with not even a twinge in the injured knee. He was able to cut for the basket and keep up with his man all the way. The first time he handled the ball, however, was on a pass from Mackey as Ron broke for the basket. The pass was good but not as good as it might have been. Ron had to stretch for the ball, and in stretching he was off balance and unable to get his shot up toward the basket. He had to pass out to Sterovitch.

The Turbines moved the ball around, looking for the

openings, trying to set up a screen. Ron wondered about Mackey's pass as he worked the ball with the others. Was the same thing happening with all of the Turbine players? Were most of Jig's passes just a trifle "off" and a little difficult to handle? Was Mackey's man occasionally getting the half-step on him?

It was very hard to tell because this was a subtle thing. A skilled court man could easily slough off in this manner with no one the wiser, unless he was watched constantly, and started to tip his hand.

At half-time the Boxers had closed the gap and it was 51-51 when the teams left the floor. As far as Ron could see Mackey had done nothing really wrong. He'd missed a lay-up now and then but so had everybody else, Ron included. This could happen to any man.

In the score book Ron noticed, also, that Mackey had outscored the man he was guarding by two points. Jig had fourteen points for the half, a very creditable performance. Could a man play that kind of game and still play to lose? Reluctantly, Ron Starrett had to admit that he *could!*

"We're still not sharp," Bo McCloud said in the dressing room. "We should be a dozen points ahead of this bunch."

Ron glanced at Jig Mackey across the room. Jig was sitting with his back against the wall, looking up at the ceiling, his handsome face sweaty. Bennie Andrews sat near him, studying his shoelaces.

Ron started the second half in place of Bennie, who was fighting a cold and whose shooting, for once, was off. While on the court now Ron watched Mackey every possible moment, even though he realized how difficult it was, trying to pin-point anything like this.

On one occasion Mackey hooked his man going up toward the rim for a shot and the Boxer player made two free throws. It was impossible to say whether Jig could have blocked the shot with a legal maneuver. Again a Mackey pass got away from Moynihan, but had Jig's pass really been too hot to handle or had Stretch just bobbled it?

All the way it was uninspired basketball and the Turbine crowd was not too happy about it. Near the end of the third period Ron pulled Jig out of the game, putting Doug Maceo in for him. Still there was no noticeable improvement. Doug just wasn't the floorman to take Jig's place, and after Doug lost the ball to a Boxer player a disgruntled fan in the balcony yelled loudly,

"What's the matter, Starrett? Don't you know how to coach a team? Get Jig back in there."

In the fourth period, with the Boxers leading 88-82, Ron put Jig back in again but still they weren't clicking. Bo McCloud went on a one-man rampage, picking up six straight points, but then the Boxers began to pull away again.

Mackey missed a set shot from the corner and the Boxers took the ball. They scored and then scored again.

Ron went out, putting Bennie Andrews back in, but the play was still rough. This was no longer the smooth-functioning team which had taken the Ironmen that opening game. They were losing the ball, constantly losing the ball, but Jig Mackey was *scoring!*

It was Mackey who brought the team back to within hailing distance of the Boxers. Jig hit with a beautiful lay-up as he cut under the basket; he scored again from outside with a set shot, and then added another point on a free throw with the crowd cheering him on.

It was 96-95 for the Boxers with less than a minute remaining when the Boxers started a freeze. Bo McCloud, though, smashed through to bat the ball away from his man.

Ron scooped up the loose ball and the Turbine crowd roared as he sprinted upcourt with his man slanting over to pick him up. Out of the corner of his eye he saw Mackey sprinting toward the basket. He could have gone all the way on the play, trying a driving lay-up down the middle, but Jig was in the clear and, automatically, Ron whipped the ball to him.

Mackey's man was closing in on him but he still had time to get off his shot. Instead of shooting, though, he passed off to Bo, who was coming up behind the play as a trailer.

Surprised at the unexpected pass, when he'd thought Jig was going to shoot, Bo juggled the ball and a big Boxer player batted it away. Another Boxer picked it up and the game was over.

There were boos from the seats as the Turbines walked off the court, having lost their third game in a row.

In the dressing room, Bo McCloud was ready to tear his uniform to pieces.

"I bobbled the easy one," he moaned. "The real easy one."

"Everybody misses them," Stretch tried to console him. "You made plenty tonight, Bo."

"Not the big one," Bo said glumly.

Ron sat on the edge of the bench wiping his wet face with a towel. He watched Mackey walking down toward the shower room. What really had happened on that play? Jig had passed off when he'd had a reasonably good shot at the rim, thus perhaps losing the game, but he, himself, had passed off to Mackey when he could have taken a shot. How could he accuse Jig? Besides, Jig had been high scorer tonight, with thirty-three points.

Disheartened, Ron left Union Hall with Millicent. His Kilowatt Kids had played in the opener against a high-school jayvee squad, licking them by a nice margin, and Ron felt quite happy about that, but the Turbines had lost three in a row and the Atlas supporters were becoming more and more disgruntled.

"I wouldn't worry," Millicent tried to cheer him. "You did the best you could, Ron."

Ron shook his head. He was the coach and he had to bear the responsibility. The Turbines were using his system, his set plays and fast breaks. It didn't do any good trying to pass the buck.

"I'm not the most popular man in Willmantic City these days," he said glumly as they drove downtown. "If someone were to put on a popularity contest, I'd surely come in last."

"Now you're feeling sorry for yourself," Millicent chided. "That's not like you, Ron. Snap out of it."

At the plant the next day Adam Greer, seeing Ron in the corridor, said, "What's happening to our basketball team, Ron? Can't you jolt them out of this slump?"

"I'm not sure what it is," Ron admitted, "except that we're not winning, Mr. Greer."

Adam Greer frowned. "I'd hoped to have a good team this year," he said. "It means a lot to the company by way of morale. I suppose you've heard that there is a petition going around asking for your removal?"

Ron stared at the superintendent, sick at heart. He hadn't realized that things were *that* bad as yet. "I'm sorry about it," he said slowly.

The thought of losing his job at Atlas hadn't really occurred to him, but now it was a distinct possibility. Adam Greer had a right to expect that his team, one of the few in the league with a full-time coach, would proudly represent Atlas Power and Light. The Turbines weren't doing that at all, and he still didn't know the reason.

Was it Mackey? Was Jig taking gamblers' bribe money,

and, if so, could they possibly catch him at it? Otherwise, things could go on this way the remainder of the season with Jig sloughing off and helping them lose every game.

"I'm terribly sorry things aren't working out," Ron said slowly.

"You play the Wheelers Friday night, do you not?" Mr. Greer asked.

"That's right," Ron nodded.

"Let's get back into the win column," the superintendent told him. "We've beaten this team before in an exhibition game. We should be able to do it again."

The Turbines had beaten the Wheelers before they'd had a coach. If they couldn't beat them now *with* a coach, then obviously something was wrong with the coach. Ron could feel the pressure on him and it wasn't very pleasant.

In the company garage that afternoon he mentioned the matter of the petition to Stretch Moynihan and Bo McCloud.

"Heard about it," Stretch said tersely, "an' I nearly punched one guy's nose in when he asked me if I wanted to sign. These guys in the seats don't know what's goin' on down on the floor."

"They know we're losing," Ron told him, "and they want me out. I surely didn't come here to be a hindrance to the team."

"Don't be crazy," Bo put in quickly. "This stuff you showed us is good, solid basketball, an' you've been playin' a crackerjack game, yourself."

"Except against the Rockets," Ron observed dryly.

"That Magruder is liable to kick anybody around the first time out," Stretch told him. "It don't mean a thing. We'll start winnin' soon."

Ron wasn't too sure. If somebody on the squad was playing to lose, the Turbines would never start winning. That was obvious.

He'd scheduled another practice session for the following evening and it was a good workout. This he couldn't understand, either. The team looked great in practice sessions. All the plays worked flawlessly. The passing was sharp and accurate.

When the workout was over, Ron followed the players into the dressing room. He had a few words with Bo McCloud near the door and then moved on toward his locker. Walking down the narrow aisle between the lockers, he noticed that one of the doors was open. A pair of sneakers lay on the floor in front of the locker, the player evidently having gone on to the shower room.

As Ron moved past the open locker he saw a postcard on the floor just beneath the bench. Bending down to pick it up, he saw that it was a call card from the Willmantic Library, advising that a requested book was available. The addressee was asked to stop in for it.

The title of the book was *Basketball Coaching Techniques,* and it was by A. B. Sillinger, a top collegiate coach. Ron knew it well.

Curiously, he turned the postcard over, wondering who

could have ordered it. He stared at the card. It was addressed to George Mackey.

Ron stood in the aisle with the card in his hand. If Mackey was reading books on coaching techniques, this meant that Mackey was interested in coaching basketball. But where? Atlas Power had just signed on a basketball coach. Was Jig interested in coaching at *Atlas?*

A light began to dawn on Ron. The pieces began to fit together. If Jig did hope to coach the Turbines, the only way he could do it would be to get rid of the present coach, and the way the team was going he seemed well on the road to success. With Jig sloughing off so that the Turbines lost steadily, the company as well as the Willmantic fans would become disillusioned with the new collegiate star. Bennie Andrews had suspected that Jig was throwing games, but Bennie didn't know the reason. Now, Ron realized that Jig had a motive and a very solid one.

Slowly, Ron replaced the card on the locker-room floor and then walked on to his own locker. He remembered now that Jig had made suggestions in the Ironman game. Jig knew his basketball and possibly he'd hoped to get the coaching position even before the company had called Ron to the scene. Disappointed, was he now undermining Ron, seeing to it that the Turbines lost and lost again, with no one ever suspecting one of the bright stars of the team? Only the veteran Bennie Andrews, who'd played with Jig a long time, had begun questioning Jig's game.

Of course Ron still didn't have any kind of proof. He

could not go to Adam Greer with a postcard from the Willmantic Library and tell him that Jig's dogging it was the reason the Turbines were losing. He was going to watch Jig, though, in the next game, watch him like a hawk, and this time he would know!

13

Big Abe Kindred and his Wheeler teammates with the golden sneakers and the gaudy green and gold sweat-suits arrived in Willmantic two nights later.

"Tonight," Rocco said grimly in the dressing room, "we break that losing streak."

Ron looked around the room. Mackey was adjusting the laces of his shoes in front of his locker. He was very calm, his face expressionless.

Tonight, Ron thought bitterly, *we'll find out.*

As the Turbines stepped out on the court ten minutes later Ron knew very definitely that the crowd was no longer behind the team as it had been that opening night. When he stepped up to the foul line to take a few practice throws he was booed roundly, and this hurt. He told himself that they had to win this game; he had to prove to Adam Greer that he could handle an industrial league team.

Because Bennie Andrews now had a full-fledged cold and wasn't in the best of shape, Ron decided to start himself with the other regulars, and immediately that this became known a group of partisan Turbine rooters began to chant loudly,

"We want Bennie! We want Bennie."

Resolved to make good despite the booing, Ron went in fast on the tap and took the ball away from a Wheeler player. He shot it across to McCloud and the Turbines moved upcourt.

Going across the ten-second line, Ron lifted two fingers to set up one of the pick-offs. Sterovitch whipped the ball to McCloud. Jig Mackey was supposed to move up behind Bo's man. Then when Bo passed the ball out and made his cut, the Wheeler player guarding him would find himself entangled with Mackey behind him. The play was designed to give Bo the step to the basket with the feed pass coming from Ron.

Bo fired the ball out to Ron and then cut, swinging around behind Mackey. The play didn't work, though, because the man Mackey was supposed to screen out seemed to get by Jig without too much trouble, knocking down Ron's loop pass to McCloud.

Ron's brown eyes flicked. He fell back toward his own basket, picking up his man as he went. It was Mackey's man, too, who made the first score for the Wheelers. Jig seemed to be caught in a bind under the basket as his man spun away with a hook shot. Mackey lunged after him desperately, but too late, a trifle too late. It was 2-0 for the Wheelers.

Moynihan tied it up with a shot from the bucket and then McCloud pushed in a lay-up. Ron, taking a bounce pass from Sterovitch, dropped in another lay-up and the team was beginning to look good. But then the trouble Ron had been anticipating started.

A pass from Jig got away from Rocco Sterovitch and the Wheelers recovered the ball. Working a fast break, Abe Kindred dropped in a two-pointer.

A short while later another Mackey bounce pass to Moynihan was intercepted by a Wheeler player. Ron's eyes hardened. It was coming into focus now. When you wanted to see it you could see it. When you were looking for it, it was there!

Mackey scored on a lay-up, another of his scintillating plays, but when a short while later he tried a feed pass to McCloud cutting for the rim, the ball grazed Bo's finger-tips. It seemed that Jig's passes were often a trifle ahead of the receiver, or just a bit too hard to handle. The ball went out of bounds and the Wheelers took possession.

Calling for time, Ron walked to the bench for a towel. He said tersely as the other four men came up to him, "Let's watch that careless passing."

Mackey was standing a few feet away. He turned and looked at Ron quickly, but he said nothing.

The Turbines took the ball under their own basket, put it in play, and a moment later Jig Mackey electrified the crowd with a sensational one-hand shot as he took a pass from McCloud directly under the basket, kept going, and flipped the ball over his head as he was moving. It was by far the best shot of the evening and the Turbine crowd roared in approval.

On a switch a short while later, though, as Mackey was guarding Rocco's man, the Wheeler player got away from Jig and netted an easy two-pointer.

His face set tight, Ron took the ball out of bounds, throwing it in to McCloud. The Turbines moved up-court, Mackey, as usual, remaining in the rear to feed the ball to the players making the cuts.

Ron called for another set play, this one revolving around Moynihan in the bucket. Bo, coming up behind big Stretch's man, stationed himself solidly. The ball was to go in to Moynihan, out to Ron, over to Mackey, who was then to feed McCloud as Bo swung in around the front of Moynihan, the stationary block.

McCloud had the step on his man as the Wheeler guarding him had to work around Moynihan, but Mackey's pass was a little ahead of him so that Bo, instead of getting off the shot, had to move the ball out again to Ron. The pass had not actually been bad, but Bo had been unable to make his shot.

Turning with the ball in his hand, Ron said to the referee, "Time."

He tossed the ball away, walked toward the bench, and said to Georgie Kramer, "O.K., George. You're in for Mackey."

Kramer, surprised, stepped up to the scorer's table. As the Turbine regulars came in, Ron said to Mackey, "You're out, Jig."

Mackey stared at him, hands on hips, and then he looked up toward the roof of the hall in evident disgust and amazement as he came off the court to pick up his sweat jacket.

The crowd had been watching curiously, wondering why Ron had suddenly called time. When they saw Mackey walking toward the bench, a roar of protest went up.

The other players were watching curiously, all except Bennie Andrews. Bennie yelled from the bench, "Let's start to roll now, gang! A new team out there."

Ron glanced toward the seat where Adam Greer sat, seeing the grim expression on the Atlas superintendent's face as the booing continued.

The noise seemed to unsettle the Turbines, too, as they put the ball in play. Anxious to make good, they pressed. A pass got away from Moynihan and the Wheelers had the ball and were moving fast upcourt with it.

Ron picked up Rocco's man who was in the clear and cutting for the basket. It was a two-on-one as another Wheeler stormed down the middle. The first man pulled back, received a pass, and braced himself for a set shot.

Determined to block the shot at any cost, Ron rushed toward him, going up very high, committing himself long before the Wheeler player took the shot, and only when he had both feet off the floor realizing that he'd been fooled.

Grinning, the Wheeler player faked his set shot and

dribbled around Ron in toward the basket for an easy lay-up. Ron didn't remember when he'd looked so foolish in his life. He'd been high in the air, arms and legs spread, reaching for a shot which never came.

Now the crowd roared and the remarks coming down from the balcony were highly uncomplimentary.

"Go back to college, you bum!" one man howled.

Another group started to chant, "We want Mackey! We want Mackey!"

Rocco, seeing Ron's face, said, "Take it easy, kid. Don't let 'em get you."

At the end of the period, with the score 21-18 for the Wheelers, Ron took himself out and put Bennie Andrews into the game. He'd scored four points in the period.

Sitting down on the bench Ron pulled his sweat jacket around his shoulders and mopped his face with a towel. Adam Greer sat a few rows behind the bench, his eyes hard. Jig Mackey sat at the far end of the bench, the look of the martyr on his face as the crowd continued to chant, "We want Mackey."

Ron paid no attention to them. He sat next to Doug Maceo and he watched the five Turbines on the floor. Bennie Andrews was trying desperately to straighten them out. Little Bennie was going all out, fighting for him, trying to make it look all right, but the Turbines were mixed up. McCloud, Moynihan and Sterovitch still didn't know what had happened. Kramer, in for Mackey, wasn't too happy about this constant chanting for Jig.

Because they had this on their minds it was reflected in the play of the men. They played stolid, uninspired basketball while the Wheelers, realizing that they had the Turbines on the ropes, pressed all the harder, breaking faster than ever when they got possession of the ball, pulling ahead to a 55-40 lead at half-time.

Bennie scored ten points in the short while that he was in the game, but, although Bennie was all over the court trying to rally the team, it wasn't enough. With the crowd still booing lustily Ron followed his team off the court and down the corridor to the dressing room.

Jig Mackey waited until Ron came up to him and then he said tersely, "Why was I benched, Starrett?"

Ron looked at him. "Don't you know?" he asked, his voice tight.

"You tell me," Jig countered.

Ron pulled up in the corridor.

"I'll tell you," he said bitterly. "You're not playing to win, Mackey, and you haven't been playing to win since the Ironman game when you decided you were going to have me dumped as coach."

Jig licked his lips. "Why would I want you dumped?" he asked.

"Because you want the job yourself," Ron told him.

Jig was staring at him. "That's ridiculous," he said. "You're just talking, Starrett. The team is going to pot and you're trying to blame me. I dare you to go to Mr. Greer with that story."

Ron's face was pale with anger. "You know I can't do that," he snapped. "You know you have me over a barrel."

"O.K.," Jig said coolly. "Then bench me."

He walked off. Bennie Andrews, coming out of the locker room, passed Mackey on the way in, giving him a hard stare as he did so. When Ron came up, Bennie said quietly,

"So you saw it, too?"

"I saw it," Ron nodded.

"You think he's shaving points?" Bennie asked. "Taking gamblers' money?"

Ron shook his head. "I think he's after my job," he stated, and then he explained about the library notice.

Bennie frowned. "You could never prove anything with that postcard," he pointed out. "It would be your word against his. Of course I'll stand behind you, Ron. Maybe some of the other guys will start remembering also, that Jig's play did look a little funny at times. But what are you going to do now? Are you going to bench him the rest of the season?"

Ron laughed grimly. "I can't play him if I know he's dogging it," he said. "What's the use of even putting a team on the floor when you know one man is working against it?"

"And if you bench him," Bennie observed, "that crowd out there will have your hide. Besides, Adam Greer's going to have you on the carpet after this game, anyway."

Ron knew that, also. He'd kept one of his top stars on

the bench almost the entire first half, and Mr. Greer would want an explanation for that.

Bennie said softly, "You don't have till *after* the game, Ron. Here he comes now."

Ron turned and saw the superintendent coming down the corridor, face grim, shoulders set tight.

"I'll talk to him alone, Bennie," Ron told the little Turbine player.

Mr. Greer said quietly when he pulled up in front of Ron, "It was never my intention, Ron, to interfere with you as coach of the Atlas team, but I believe you can understand why I must take some action. I think we both realize that the Atlas Turbines are a public relations phase of our work, and from what I've seen tonight these relations are becoming quite strained."

Ron nodded. "I—I'm certainly sorry the way things have been going, Mr. Greer."

"It isn't just a matter of winning or losing," Adam Greer went on, "but if the Turbines are unpopular in the Willmantic Valley, they cease to have a reason for existing."

"I can understand that," Ron told him.

"Now what's happening?" Adam Greer asked. "Why was Mackey benched for most of the first half when everybody thought he was playing excellent basketball."

Ron took a deep breath. "I'm afraid I can't tell you that right now, Mr. Greer."

The Atlas superintendent's jaw stiffened. "All right,"

he said flatly. "Possibly, I have no right to ask. You still are coach of the Turbines and you may use your own judgment as to who should play and who should not. Only remember this, Starrett, if the team continues to lose and you are so unpopular with our people that they have to get up a petition to fire you, then I'm afraid I'll have to ask for your resignation."

He turned and walked off, and Ron, watching him go, felt sick at heart. He was remembering how bright things had been after that Ironman win. He had a future in the Willmantic Valley, then, a future with Atlas Power, and he'd met a wonderful girl. Now probably all was gone.

Turning, he walked into the Turbine dressing room feeling as low as he'd ever felt in his life. A silent, grim-faced Turbine team watched him.

Jig Mackey lay on the rubbing table, looking up at the ceiling. Bo McCloud sat with Rocco Sterovitch. Moynihan was looking in the mirror at a bruise on his cheekbone.

McCloud said uncertainly, "We gotta get goin', gang."

Rocco said, "Let's everybody fight for that ball. *Fight* for it."

Ron didn't say anything until they were about to go out on the floor and then he announced the line-up which would start the second half. Mackey was still on the bench. Ron was in the game along with Bennie Andrews.

"We can make it a ball game," he finished. "We've beaten this team before."

He waited now at the door as the players filed out. Mackey went first, a very faint smile on his face, the triumph in his dark eyes. Bo McCloud came last, pausing in front of Ron. He said hesitantly, "You're the coach, Ron. It's no business of mine but ain't you startin' Jig?"

"No," Ron said and he left it there.

14

As the Turbines came out on the court for the second half the crowd immediately began to boo lustily. When the five Turbine players stripped off their sweat jackets and it was known that Jig Mackey still wasn't playing, the booing became even more vicious.

A fan leaned down out of the balcony and whooped, "What's the matter with Mackey, you bum?"

Ron did not even look up. He had already had a glimpse of Millicent Brown's tense face as she sat next to the grim Adam Greer.

The half got under way with the Turbines playing good, solid basketball, but they had a fifteen point deficit to make up. Moynihan started the scoring in the second half with a nice lay-up from the bucket, and then McCloud, driving in from the corner, took Ron's feed pass and netted the ball for another two-pointer.

The Wheelers, however, had the scent of victory in their nostrils and they weren't quitting. Besides, big Abe Kindred was having a night of nights. Abe was netting the ball with either hand from the pivot spot, some of them long, sweeping shots which were impossible to stop.

He was hitting tonight the way he'd never hit in his life.

Desperately, the Turbines strove to catch up. They came to within five points, and then three points, of the Wheelers, going into the fourth period, but invariably Kindred would make the big sweep and come in with a one-hander.

Despite the considerably better play on the part of the Turbines, the crowd was still resentful. There were occasional cheers as the home team crept up, but Mackey's benching seemed to have embittered a great many of the Turbine rooters. Mackey had been one of their favorites, a picture player, a floorman, never a ball hog, and they'd liked him.

Every once in a while the chant would begin again: "We want Mackey!"

Near the end Bennie Andrews began to feel the pace, and Ron replaced him with Doug Maceo. It was 85-80 for the Wheelers. Sterovitch hit from the corner; McCloud tipped in a rebound; Moynihan hit with a free throw and the score was tied. It was the first time all evening that the Turbine crowd really perked up, but it didn't last.

Abe Kindred, who'd already scored forty-three points, dropped in another field goal. Moynihan, battling desperately, matched him with a tip-in, and then Ron hit from the corner with a set shot.

The Wheelers roared back with two quick field goals. With a minute remaining the Turbines had a chance to tie it up again but Ron's lay-up was knocked down by

Abe Kindred. The Wheelers took the ball and froze till the gun went off. It was 91-89 for the Wheelers and the Turbines had lost their fourth in a row.

The team left the court amidst the loudest booing Ron Starrett had ever heard, and it wasn't for the Turbines. It was for *him*.

As he was going into the tunnel under the balcony a loud-voiced fan roared, "Somebody get me that petition. I'll sign it now, boys!"

Ron was wondering bitterly about the petition as he followed his team down the corridor. Possibly, Jig had surreptitiously rigged that up, also. It would have been very easy for him to start something like that going around. The more Ron thought about it the more he was convinced that Mackey *was* behind the petition, but again —the proof. There was no proof whatever.

Ron walked into the Turbine dressing room just as Bennie Andrews was stepping up to Jig Mackey, his face white with rage. Bennie was nearly a head shorter than Mackey and a dozen years older but it looked for a moment as if Bennie was going to swing at the taller man.

"What do you mean I don't know what I'm talking about?" Bennie yelled. "You're dogging it out there, Mackey. You've been throwing games since we played the Rockets."

"That's—that's crazy," Mackey spluttered. "You're out of your head, Bennie."

Ron had a look at Mackey's eyes and he saw the fear in

them. It suddenly occurred to him that Jig was a coward, a contemptuous coward. Any man who would do what he'd been doing was not much of a man. Maybe that weakness in him could be exploited.

Bo McCloud had gotten up from the bench nearby and come over to where Mackey and Andrews were standing.

"How about this?" Bo asked tersely. "Bennie don't talk through his hat, Jig."

"It—it's crazy!" Jig insisted. "I don't even know what he's talking about."

Bo looked at Ron. "That the reason you benched Jig, Ron, because you figured he wasn't playin' to win?"

Ron took a deep breath. "That's the reason," he said grimly. "He's been throwing games ever since we beat the Ironmen."

Jig Mackey backed away, breathing deeply. "You guys are trying to gang up on me," he gasped. "Why would I want to throw games?"

"To get me out of here," Ron told him flatly. "You want my job as coach on this team. That's the reason you started that petition, too."

Rocco Sterovitch was standing up, face dark with anger. "I'm beginnin' to remember," he said softly, "how a lot of your passes kept gettin' away from me, Jig. Maybe they just weren't thrown so good. Is that it?"

Stretch Moynihan had gotten up, also. "You scored plenty, Mackey," he said slowly, "but never when we needed the points to win. How come?"

Mackey was trying to swallow. "That's just—just talk," he spluttered.

Ron said quietly, "I have the proof that you're the one who started the petition to have me fired, Mackey. I have the proof right here in my coat pocket."

He opened his locker nearby and took out a few envelopes. The letters were really from amateur junior teams from outside the Valley with whom he'd been trying to arrange exhibition games for his Kilowatt Kids.

Jig Mackey stared at the packet of letters, his face white now.

"When I show these to Mr. Greer," Ron said tersely, "you're finished at Atlas, Mackey."

Jig Mackey was staring at him. "I—I'll be fired," he whispered. "Look, Ron, it—it was only a joke. The petition didn't mean anything. I—I—"

Bo McCloud broke in on him. "*You* started that petition?" he asked, his face red.

Jig gulped again and looked at the letters in Ron's hand. "It was only a joke," he said lamely.

Rocco Sterovitch said slowly, distinctly, "Mackey, get out of here. We don't want to see your kind around here any more."

After he'd gone, Bo said to Ron, "Some of us are goin' to see Mr. Greer in the morning, Ron. We'll get this whole mess straightened out."

"When I think back on it," Stretch Moynihan mused, "I can remember half a dozen different times when Jig fouled things up on us during a game. He was the last guy you'd suspect, though, and none of us were looking for it."

Bennie Andrews said curiously to Ron, "I didn't know you had proof that Jig was behind that petition."

"I didn't," Ron admitted. "It was all bluff, Bennie."

"It sure worked," Bennie smiled. "Jig looked like the roof had fallen in on him when you pulled out those letters."

"What do you think he'll do?" Ron asked curiously.

"He'll run now," Bennie said with conviction. "If I know Mackey, he'll just pull out."

Bennie's prediction proved true. In the morning after a delegation of Turbine players had called on Adam Greer, Ron was asked to come in to the office.

The Atlas superintendent shook hands with him warmly. "I'm terribly sorry about the whole mess, Ron," he stated. "There's no doubt in my mind, whatever, that Mackey was playing against you. As a matter of fact, he quit this morning, asked for his paycheck, and walked out without even coming in to see me. I do hope things work out better for you now."

"I hope so, too," Ron said with a smile. "I really want to settle down at Atlas, Mr. Greer."

There was a shadow in the superintendent's gray eyes. "I suppose you realize, though, that you're still not out of the woods, Ron, as far as the Atlas fans are concerned. You'll still have to prove yourself to them."

Ron knew that, also, and he was going to have to do it against the Allegheny Rockets in three days. It wasn't a very pleasant prospect.

Millicent Brown spoke to him before he left the office to report to the pump room where he was now working.

"I've heard the news," Millicent said warmly. "I'm so very pleased that you're cleared, Ron."

"So am I," Ron told her. "It certainly was awful."

"We're not going to say too much about the Mackey business," Millicent went on, "because it's not too good as a matter of public relations, but the word will begin to spread sooner or later as to why Mackey is no longer with the team. They'll accept you."

They'll accept me, Ron was thinking, *when I prove to them that I'm able to hold down this coaching job, and when we start to win—beginning with the Rockets!*

"I'm very glad you're staying with us," Millicent said softly.

Ron looked at her. "You can't be any happier than I," he said truthfully.

He felt as if a great load had been lifted from his back.

15

All of the Turbine players were in the dressing room when Ron entered the night of the Allegheny game. The moment he came into the room, however, he noticed the glum expressions on their faces.

"Anything wrong?" he asked quickly.

Rocco Sterovitch looked over at Stretch Moynihan who was sitting on the bench nearby, long legs extended, arms folded across his chest, face creased in a frown.

"Ask that big baboon," Rocco said grimly.

"I can play," Moynihan said flatly.

"Sure," Rocco retorted, "an' so can Santy Claus, but not good."

"What happened?" Ron asked, knowing instinctively that his short spell of good luck was about to run out.

"Stretch kind of wrenched his back this afternoon," Rocco explained. "Nearly took a fall from a pole. He caught himself but he's got a pretty bad back."

"I can play," Moynihan said.

Ron looked at him, knowing what Stretch meant to this team. The Turbines needed the big fellow under the boards to help control the ball. Without him, the burden would be upon Sterovitch and McCloud, and neither was an exceptionally big man.

"I'd like to start, Ron," Stretch told him. "I might work this thing out."

Ron nodded. "We'll see how it goes," he said and he sat down in front of his locker to change, wondering why it had to be this way. If the Turbines took another bad drubbing tonight from the Rockets, he would still not have the confidence of the Atlas rooters. With or without Mackey, the new coach from the collegiate ranks would not have it in this rough and tough league.

Bennie Andrews said quietly, "We've got to take this bunch tonight, Ron."

"I know," Ron agreed.

"Stretch will kill himself out on the court," Bennie went on, "but I don't think he'll have it. You must be a kangaroo under that basket, and these Rockets have terrific rebound men."

"I'll start him," Ron said. "I know how he feels about this game after what they did to us the last time. If Stretch doesn't have it, I'll put Kramer in right away."

When the Turbines trotted out on the floor, Ron leading them, there was the usual chorus of boos. When it became apparent that Mackey was not even in uniform, a buzz of talk went through the hall.

The Rockets were down at the far end of the court in their orange and black outfits, very confident, very sure of themselves, unbeaten this season, with seven straight wins, and obviously heading toward another industrial league title.

The knowledge that the Atlas Turbines seemed to have been shot through with dissension and had lost the support of the town gave the Rockets even more confidence. They would be playing loose and easy tonight, and a loose and easy team was usually a hard one to beat.

Ron took a set shot, missed it, and someone in the crowd booed.

Rocco said, "Don't worry about it, kid. They paid their dollar an' they got a right to boo in this league."

Ron just nodded but his jaw was tight as the teams lined up for the opening tap. He had his regulars on the floor with big Stretch at the center position.

Studs Magruder said to him as they moved to their positions, "What are you doin', Starrett, *losin'* a popularity contest?"

Ron didn't answer him. He knew that tonight he had to hold this man, hold him every step of the way. He had to play him all night and he had to hold him. And he had to score, himself, because the Turbines probably would be losing the services of Stretch Moynihan.

Ron went in fast at the tap, reached for the ball, came down with it, and then had it batted away by the quick hands of Studs Magruder. A Rocket player scooped it up and the league leaders sped downcourt confidently.

Desperately, Ron took after Magruder who was cutting in for the basket. He blocked Studs's lay-up but the referee called a holding foul on him.

Magruder made both free throws and the Rockets led 2-0. With the Turbines in possession, Ron watched Stretch Moynihan moving around in the bucket. Rocco fired the ball in to Stretch and Stretch shot it out to Bennie Andrews.

Bennie bounced it to Bo cutting down the middle and Bo went high with the lay-up. The ball rolled off the rim and the tall Rocket center, Jim Lacey, came down with it. Moynihan had gone up after that rebound but the Rocket center had come down with the ball.

Studs Magruder was moving away fast and Ron went with him, matching the speedster stride for stride. Magruder feinted and cut and then he stopped suddenly, backed himself against Ron, and then cut again. Momentarily free now he took a pass, whirled, and flipped in the set shot making the score 4-0.

The boos from the seats were deafening, and Studs Magruder said to Ron as they were moving upcourt again, "You're even worse than the last time, college boy. Why don't you put somebody else to guard me?"

Ron took a pass from Rocco Sterovitch and fired the ball to Bennie Andrews. He cut in around Stretch's block and took Bennie's short pass. He kept going, driving across the center, and then lifting the ball up toward the rim with his right hand. It was a nice play but the ball didn't go through the cords.

As the ball came off the rim big Stretch went up with

the others and Ron clearly heard the big fellow's groan of pain. Lacey came down again with the rebound.

Ron chased Magruder upcourt, playing him close, and watching for those underhanded maneuvers. When Magruder moved in front of him he waited for the stomping foot. This time Magruder slyly dug an elbow in his stomach before he broke, but Ron was still with him. When Studs took a pass he made the Rocket ace move toward the sidelines away from the basket, and Studs had to pass out again.

Lacey took a pass in the bucket and went up high, higher than Stretch Moynihan, making the basket. Ron took one look at Stretch's white face and he called for time.

When the players moved over toward the Turbine bench, Ron said to the tall center, "I guess that does it, Stretch. I appreciate your trying."

Moynihan just shook his head. "I wanted to win this one for you, kid," he said dully. "I know what it means to you."

As Stretch sat down on the bench an attending physician came over to look at him. The Atlas crowd stared in amazement, remembering how Ron had benched Mackey in the previous game. The booing was loud and raucous as Georgie Kramer came out on the court.

"Let's go, George," Ron said. "Make it a game."

Kramer nodded grimly.

The whistle blew and they had to put the ball in play. Ron passed in from the outside to Rocco and they moved upcourt, Andrews to Kramer, who whipped a beautiful pass to Bo McCloud driving in from the corner. Bo's shot, however, rolled off the rim, but Kramer, following up his pass, tipped the ball back in for the two-pointer.

Sterovitch then scored with a set shot but the Rockets immediately went on a scoring spree. The Allegheny team's shooting tonight was of the highest caliber. They tried long shots and they hit. Magruder scored with a one-hander which was impossible to block. Their strong man, Mulvane, who was built like a brick wall, roared down the middle, bounced off Rocco, and made his shot.

At the end of the first period it was 21-8 for the Rockets. Bennie Andrews, panting, left the game for a breather and Doug Maceo came in. It was a comparatively small team on the floor for the Turbines, and the Rockets were controlling the boards which usually meant the game.

Ron had hit with a lay-up but Studs Magruder had scored ten points in the quarter and seemed off and flying on one of his usual hot nights. He was playing it dirty, too, elbowing Ron, pushing him and jostling him surreptitiously under the basket.

As they started the second period Studs deftly tripped Ron as he was streaking down the sidelines. Moving at top speed, Ron tumbled in among the seats along the floor. The Rockets scored a basket, but when Ron came back onto the floor shaken, bleeding from a cut lip, he noticed that Bo McCloud had called for time. Bo's face was livid with rage as he confronted Studs Magruder, giving him a tongue-lashing.

"You've pushed this kid around long enough," Bo was shouting. "You don't lay off him, I'm gonna work on you, myself."

Ron moved in front of Bo. "They'll put you out of the game, Bo," he pleaded. "Calm down."

"They have to let you play the game," Bo scowled. "They *have* to."

"Take it easy," Ron told him. "I'll handle Magruder."

Bo McCloud stood in the huddle near the Turbine bench, face still taut with anger.

"If he keeps it up," Bo said tersely, "I'm gonna break him in half after the game. I told him that, too."

"Let's win this game," Ron said. "Never mind taking care of anybody after it's over."

"They're killing us with their shooting," Georgie Kramer said glumly. "There just doesn't seem to be any way of stopping them."

"We'll have to play possession basketball," Ron said. "They can't score when they don't have the ball. We'll slow down our own shooting and hang on to the ball until we get a clear shot at the rim."

Rocco was nodding approvingly. "We been throwin' that ball away too much," he said. "Let's hang on to it until we get in there with the score."

"Keep moving the ball inside the ten-second line," Ron advised, "and no shooting from outside. Work it in close for the big one."

"O.K.," Bo said grimly. "Let's go."

At the tap Ron and Studs Magruder went in fast for the ball, and this time Ron came away with it. He shot it across to Bo and Bo passed to Doug Maceo. They crossed the ten-second line, deliberately slowing down their game but keeping the ball moving all the time.

Ron had Georgie Kramer sliding in and out of the bucket, and, while George wasn't nearly as good a man as Moynihan, he kept the ball flowing. They passed in and they passed out and they kept possession. Winning by a wide margin, the Rockets were content to let the Turbines keep the ball as long as they didn't score.

It was Ron who finally went in for the first shot coming out of this new strategy. Taking the bounce pass from McCloud, he whirled past Studs Magruder down the middle. Moving the ball away from Jim Lacey's out-stretched hand he pushed it through the cords for the two-pointer.

The strategy now was to hold the Rockets, to play them close until they lost possession of the ball, and then start those same tactics over again. The confident Rockets stormed down the court, moving the ball fast as usual, but when the rugged Mulvane missed a hook shot, Mc-Cloud picked up the rebound and fired it to Maceo.

They went upcourt, taking their time, working the ball carefully—in to Kramer, out to Ron, who threw it to Sterovitch, who sent it out again to McCloud. They criss-crossed the ball, waiting and watching for the pick-off which would set a man free for the one good, clean shot they wanted.

It was McCloud this time who had the step on his man, a play evolving around a screen Ron set up. Bo took the pass from Rocco and drove in for the lay-up.

There was a mixture of cheers and jeers from the Turbine crowd. It was the first time that the home team had scored twice in succession in this game.

A bad pass by a Rocket player gave the Turbines the ball the third time and they came upcourt again, using those delaying tactics, and this time it was Georgie Kramer who hit with a hook from the bucket. It was now 23-14 for the Rockets and Ron could see that this new style of play had considerably encouraged the Turbines. They moved more confidently, guarding very closely, anxious to get possession of the ball.

The Rockets scored, Lacey tapping one in, but the Turbines came back fast, Ron catching them by surprise, changing the tactics and rushing the ball downcourt at top speed. They had a three-on-two and Doug Maceo made the shot. They'd outscored the Rockets four baskets to one and it was a much better game all around.

Bennie Andrews came back into the game and now they started to move the ball faster, but always keeping possession. They worked it in and out, into the corners, into the bucket, and then Ron went down the middle, Studs fouling Ron on the lay-up.

Ron's shot went in and he made the free throw, also,

and the Turbine crowd began to perk up. Very definitely the home team had taken the play away from the Rockets, stopping their drive and starting one of their own.

During a time out Bo said with satisfaction, "We got 'em worried now, Ron. We keep puttin' the pressure on 'em an' they might crack."

"Get the ball," Ron smiled. "Get it and hang on to it. The scoring will take care of itself."

The Rockets, realizing what the Turbine team was doing, tried to counter their play with an all-court press, but this left men in the clear and the Turbines were quick to take advantage of this fact.

Rocco fired the ball to Bennie Andrews. Bennie bounced it to McCloud, cutting from the opposite corner, and Bo went up high to net the ball again. Shortly thereafter Bennie was fouled in the act of shooting and awarded two free throws, making both.

Now the Turbine crowd began to shout. The booing had stopped altogether as they watched this renewed Turbine team battling its way back into the game.

There was more scoring on both sides, the Rockets coming on hard again, and at half-time it was 38-29, a nine point spread, the exceedingly low score being attributable entirely to the slowing-down tactics of the Turbines.

"It's workin'," Rocco Sterovitch said happily in the dressing room.

"We're doing all right," Ron told him. "I think we can

catch them."

"We have to catch them," Rocco said tersely. "This game we're gonna win, kid."

"You said it," Bo scowled.

"I wish I could do something," big Stretch said.

"Don't worry about it," Ron told him.

"The next half," Bo observed, "this bunch will be crowdin' us, hopin' to make it a runaway. They'll be pushin' too hard. We watch for the loose balls."

As the team went back on the court Ron noticed there was no booing at all. Only nine points separated the two teams, and while it was a Rocket lead, everyone in Union Hall knew that the Turbines had taken the play away from the Rockets in that second period.

Ron had Georgie Kramer at center and the other regulars back on the floor at the tap. Studs Magruder said to Ron before the jump, "What kind of basketball is this, Starrett? Why don't you guys open up?"

"Plenty of time," Ron told him.

At the tap Studs had a hand on Ron's shirt as both men raced in for the ball, but little Bennie cut in front of Studs to take possession. The Turbines moved upcourt at the same leisurely pace, flipping the ball back and forth with Georgie Kramer moving into the bucket. Ron took a pass in the corner, had an easy set shot, but preferred firing the ball outside again to work it in closer.

As he moved under the basket Studs Magruder went with him, pushing him surreptitiously. Bo lobbed the ball in to Ron when Studs for the moment was paying too much attention to Ron and not the ball. Ron caught the ball and flipped it up to the basket for another two-pointer. It was a "sleeper" play, seldom successful against experienced basketball players.

"Lucky," Studs muttered. He came back with a fast basket of his own, driving in from the right corner as Ron switched to pick up Bo's man. Studs's lay-up was good and it was 40-31 for the Rockets.

Very shortly thereafter, however, Bennie Andrews added another two-pointer on a lay-up as he went in under Lacey's outstretched hand. It was a new Turbine team on the floor now, a confident team, and each moment they were getting better, moving the ball around the court with precision, the passes fast, sharp and accurate. The tempo seemed to be increasing all the time and the delighted Turbine crowd was buzzing with excitement.

Ron whipped the ball in to Georgie Kramer. Georgie handed it to McCloud going across the front of him, and Bo, heading toward the corner, fired a rifle shot to Sterovitch in under the basket. Rocco made the two-pointer and it was 40-35, a five-point spead.

The disgruntled Studs Magruder, finding himself hampered because the Rockets so infrequently had the ball, played Ron rougher and rougher. On one occasion the referee caught him red-handed working an elbow into Ron's stomach, and Ron was awarded a free throw which he made good.

The Turbines crept up to within two points of the Rockets with the score 54-52 at the end of the third period, and then the Rockets scored two quick field goals, Lacey coming in with the big sweep, and Mulvane laying it down the middle. Ron stuck with Studs Magruder every moment that the Rockets had the ball, crowding him. The Rocket ace had made only two points in the third period, and it was this more than anything else which stopped the Rocket drive.

The big crowd watched the play between the two men, and with each passing moment it was becoming more and more evident that Ron had contained Studs despite Magruder's underhanded tactics.

When Studs was taken out for a breather Ron went out, also, putting Chuck Abrams into the game, and when Studs came back Ron inserted himself again. If any Turbine rooters were still laboring under the delusion that Ron was afraid to play against Magruder, they realized now that they'd been wrong.

With the Rockets leading 58-52, Ron streaked in from the left side, taking a lead pass from Bennie Andrews up high and crashing into the solid Mulvane who'd switched to pick him up. He netted the ball for the two-pointer and was awarded the extra free-throw. He walked to the line, a little shaken from the collision with Mulvane, but he made the foul throw and the Rocket lead had been cut to three points.

Bennie Andrews dropped in a set shot a few moments

later and it was now 58-57 for the Rockets, with the Turbine crowd roaring in approval and stamping on the wooden floor.

During a time out, Bo McCloud said jubilantly, "We got 'em on the run. Let's keep 'em runnin'."

"Don't get careless," Ron warned. "Make every shot count or don't try it at all. Keep the ball."

It was Bennie Andrews who put them ahead. Bennie went in from the corner, taking the feed from Sterovitch and maneuvering the ball up and around restraining hands. The Rockets came back fast and hard, grimly determined to maintain their unbeaten string. They stormed the basket, their big men driving hard now, and Rocco, McCloud and Georgie Kramer battled desperately for the rebounds. The hard-jawed Sterovitch was playing the game of his life tonight, as had all the others once they'd gotten straightened out after the disastrous first period.

Now the Turbines came swinging down the court, Ron taking the pass from McCloud, dribbling, passing off to Andrews. Bennie whipped it in to Kramer in the bucket. Ron slid across the front of Kramer, cutting toward the middle with the ball and then bouncing it to McCloud. Bo feinted his man out of position and drove in toward the basket, passing off to Kramer. Georgie's shot was good and the Turbines led by three, 61-58.

Now the Rockets came back with Studs Magruder hitting from outside and Mulvane scoring from the corner with the hook. They had a one point lead. Mc-Cloud tied it up with a free throw, with the crowd going mad and with the score seesawing back and forth.

With two minutes remaining it was 72-all. The Rockets called time. Moving back toward the Turbine bench, Ron noticed that every spectator in the hall was standing up. He'd been conscious for five minutes now of this steady, roaring sound from the seats. As he stood in front of the Turbine bench, wiping his face with the towel, he realized that it was for *them*. There were no more boos. This crowd was solidly behind them, the way they'd been behind the Turbines at the start of the season, and they were solidly behind *him!*

He looked back at Adam Greer, noticing that the superintendent was clapping and applauding with the others, a broad smile on his face.

Stretch came out on the floor and he said, "Get that ball, hang on to it, and make your last shot good."

The Rockets had possession outside and they would be bringing it upcourt. If the Turbines could take the ball away from them, freeze it momentarily, and then drive in for the last big shot, the game could be theirs.

Bo said, "Watch Studs. He's gonna come in hard, Ron. He'll want to make that big basket or draw a free throw in the attempt. That'll be all they'll need."

"I'll watch him," Ron nodded.

They went back on the court. A Rocket player tossed the ball in to Studs Magruder and Studs moved upcourt carefully, passing off to Mulvane. The Rockets were hoping to stall out, also, until they went in with the big shot to put them ahead. They moved the ball inside the ten second line with Ron hugging Studs Magruder, waiting for him to make his break. He had no doubt that the Rockets had set it up that way with Magruder, their top scorer, going in.

Studs moved outside, took a pass from Mulvane, dribbled across court, and started down the side line with Ron forcing him always toward the white stripe on the outside. Now Studs cut the other way, came back in, picking up speed as he drove toward the basket.

The Rocket star was amazingly fast but Ron kept with him and when Studs went up toward the rim with the ball, Ron had a hand on it all the way, blocking the shot and doing it cleanly.

Rocco Sterovitch seemed to shoot six feet up into the air, hard elbows and knees spread, as he grabbed the ball, passing off to McCloud.

"Go!" Ron shouted and the Turbines roared upcourt with the ball with only a matter of seconds remaining now, and they had to get off this last shot.

Bennie came dribbling down the sideline, passing off to Kramer. Georgie fed it to McCloud and McCloud tore down the middle with Ron coming up behind him on the follow-up.

Two Rockets went up with Bo, hitting him in mid-air as he flipped the ball back over his head to Ron. Studs

Magruder had been trailing Ron, also, and he grabbed at Ron's right shoulder as Ron pushed the ball up toward the rim.

The referee's whistle and the gun went off simultaneously as the ball dropped through the cords for the winning score.

The Turbine crowd surged out onto the court, preventing Ron from taking the extra free throw which they didn't need. It was 74-72 for the Turbines as the enthused crowd swirled around them.

As Ron tried to work himself across the court toward the dressing room he saw Millicent Brown watching him, smiling happily. She lifted a hand to him and waved.

He saw Johnny Baker and the other Kilowatt Kids, who'd played and won an exhibition game tonight, shouting crazily, shaking their fists at him.

Bo McCloud and Stretch Moynihan were on either side of him, helping him get through. A Turbine fan roared in Ron's ear,

"You're all right, Starrett!"

"You said a mouthful," Bo yelled back at him.

"Our boy," Stretch shouted.

"All the way," Bo said with a grin.

That was the way they left the court, and it was a good way to go. Ron Starrett could not imagine a better way.